THE GUNSMITH

#78

BARBED WIRE AND BULLETS

The Gunsmith by J.R. Roberts

Macklin's Women
The Chinese Gunmen
The Woman Hunt
The Guns of Abilene
Three Guns for Glory
Leadtown
The Longhorn War
Quanah's Revenge
Heavyweight Gun
New Orleans Fire
One-Handed Gun
The Canadian Payroll
Draw to an Inside Death
Dead Man's Hand
Bandit Gold
Buckskins and Six-Guns
Silver War
High Noon at Lancaster
Bandido Blood
The Dodge City Gang
Sasquatch Hunt
Bullets and Ballots
The Riverboat Gang
Killer Grizzly
North of the Border
Eagle's Gap
Chinatown Hell
The Panhandle Search
Wildcat Roundup
The Ponderosa War
Trouble Rides a Fast Horse
Dynamite Justice
The Posse
Night of the Gila
The Bounty Women
Black Pearl Saloon
Gundown in Paradise
King of the Border
The El Paso Salt War
The Ten Pines Killer
Hell with a Pistol
Wyoming Cattle Kill
The Golden Horseman
The Scarlet Gun
Navaho Devil

Wild Bill's Ghost
The Miner's Showdown
Archer's Revenge
Showdown in Raton
When Legends Meet
Desert Hell
The Diamond Gun
Denver Duo
Hell on Wheels
The Legend Maker
Walking Dead Man
Crossfire Mountain
The Deadly Healer
The Trail Drive War
Geronimo's Trail
The Comstock Gold Fraud
Boom Town Killer
Texas Trackdown
The Fast Draw League
Showdown in Rio Malo
Outlaw Trail
Homesteader Guns
Five Card Death
Trail Drive to Montana
Trial by Fire
The Old Whistler Gang
Daughter of Gold
Apache Gold
Plains Murder
Deadly Memories
The Nevada Timber War
New Mexico Showdown
Barbed Wire and Bullets
Death Express
When Legends Die
Six Gun Justice
The Mustang Hunters
Texas Ransom
Vengeance Town
Winner Take All
Message from a Dead Man
Ride for Vengeance
The Takersville Shoot
Blood on the Land
Six-Gun Sideshow

THE GUNSMITH

#78

BARBED WIRE AND BULLETS

J.R. ROBERTS

SPEAKING VOLUMES, LLC
NAPLES, FLORIDA
2015

THE GUNSMITH
#78 BARBED WIRE AND BULLETS

ISBN 978-1-61232-681-8

For more exciting
Books, eBooks, Audiobooks and more visit us at
www.speakingvolumes.us

Chapter One

San Antonio, Texas

Spring was a good time to be in Texas. A good time to see the wild young cowboys come shagging their tough ponies in off the range after having gathered thousands of longhorn cattle from the brush country. San Antonio was the origin of the long northern drives, and it was exciting. But eight or nine months of the year, old San Antonio was a sleepy little village where chickens and pigs could be found in the plaza, and the Mexicans and the whites rubbed shoulders as if there had never been an invading Santa Anna, a crumbling Alamo with its bullet-scarred walls, or the victorious Battle of San Jacinto. Yes, Clint Adams thought, as he sat in the Alamo Saloon and played cards, San Antonio was a fine town, located on a lazy river where the children could catch frogs or minnows if they demonstrated enough patience and skill.

The Gunsmith had been playing cards all afternoon, and his winnings, while not spectacular, tallied up to nearly eighty dollars. If he could win that big every day, he'd be a wealthy man at the end of the month. But Clint knew there would also be days when luck would run against him. When he'd struggle to build so much as a pair of deuces. When luck turned sour, it was Clint's opinion that it was time to walk away from the table and try again some other day. Losers pushed their bad luck, winners pushed their good luck. Seemed to Clint that, all things being equal in terms of skill, a gambler's philosophy ought to be just that simple.

"I'll take four more cards, Clint," a man named Hoyt, who had been losing steadily for several hours, growled. "Off the top."

Hoyt was a small rancher. A big man with protruding ears and brows who was known for his nasty disposition and poor judgment as a gambler. His wife had lost their only child to a rattlesnake bite, and she had gone crazy. Hoyt drank too much, but because of his wife and child most people tolerated his foul disposition and abusive language. But the implied accusation that Clint was double-dealing off the bottom of the deck could not be overlooked.

Clint stiffened at the insult. He had never cheated at cards, and he'd be damned if he'd allow any man to suggest anything different. "I always deal off the top, Hoyt. And I always try to be a good loser. Something you should think about before you say things that could get you into deep trouble."

The man realized that he had overstepped his good sense. He forced a weak smile and mumbled, "I reckon I didn't mean what I said."

Clint did not want trouble. He'd had a lifetime of trouble as a sheriff in too many nameless towns. He understood men like Hoyt, and though he did not like them, he would give them room if he could. Only you could never let a man call you a cheat and expect to have any respect left. "Then keep your big mouth shut," Clint replied in a voice as cold as Kansas sleet.

Hoyt blushed with anger. "I lost twenty-eight dollars and most of it has been to you!"

It was a large amount of money to Hoyt, who was known to be a man with little or nothing to show for a lot of years of hard luck and tragedy. Hoyt was a loser, a fool who needed to be brought up short and told to stop feeling sorry for himself and blaming everybody and everything for his own mistakes. "If you can't afford to lose, don't play," Clint said. "That's good advice for anyone, rich or poor."

"I don't need your damned advice!" Hoyt spat. "The fact that you're good with a gun don't mean you can tell people what to do."

"My gun has nothing to do with good sense or bad."

"The hell it don't! Without your gun, you're nothing."

Clint ground his teeth together and bit back a response. In his younger days he had killed men for less, and he regretted killing enough to avoid any more of it unless pushed to the limit. Besides, Clint was accustomed to dealing with bad losers. It was his opinion that there were very few good losers outside of the professionals who knew how fickle luck could be and were able to lose money, knowing they'd eventually win it all back.

The Gunsmith stared across the table at Hoyt. "Here," he said, shoving ten dollars toward the man. "Why don't you take that and go home. Just don't expect to sit at the same table I'm sitting at again."

Hoyt stared at the money and his hand twitched. But he wouldn't take the ten dollars, and his face got redder and redder until he looked as if he were going to explode. He clenched his hands into big fists and whispered, "If you didn't have that reputation with a gun, I'd rip your head off in a fair fight."

"You might at that," Clint said, not allowing himself to be baited into a fistfight. "But life isn't always fair, is it? So take the money and get out of here before I get mad."

Hoyt grabbed the money. He stomped over to the bar and

slammed down a dollar and ordered a bottle of cheap whiskey.

"You watch him, Clint," one of the players warned. "He's fixing to get drunk, and when he does, he gets mean and sneaky."

Clint nodded. "I hope he just goes home and sobers up."

"He won't go home until he's drunk. I been to his place. Ain't nothing left but four walls, a table and a chair. He's sold everything nice his wife owned or had. Sold it or gambled it away. Ain't nothing at home for him."

"Not even a few head of cattle or horses?"

"Nothing," the man said. "Hoyt is busted except for that ten dollars you just throwed his way. And that cost him what pride he had left."

Clint scowled. "I know the story about his wife and son. But that doesn't mean a fella can call another a cheat. Besides, I didn't ask for anything except that he never join me again in a card game."

"That's what I mean," the man said. "You kilt his pride. Hoyt has always been too proud. You better watch yourself."

Clint finished his deal. He lost four dollars and knew without a doubt that Hoyt had soured his evening and his good luck. Clint played three or four more hands and lost another twenty dollars before he said, "Deal me out."

He stood up, still thirty or forty dollars ahead. That was as much money as he could earn in a week gunsmithing, though he sometimes worked for rich people who paid top dollar to have their expensive guns and rifles worked on by someone they trusted.

Clint wandered over to the bar and ordered a beer. The clock on the wall said it was almost eight o'clock, and the sun had gone down nearly two hours ago. Anita Rollins would be coming down from her room upstairs pretty soon. She'd sing and dance with a few of the other girls, and the cowboys would whoop and holler for her to show them her bare ankles. It was a routine that hardly ever varied. Clint might try his hand at roulette or he might just watch Anita and the girls and listen to Art, the piano player.

Maybe old Sheriff Gus North would be wanting to talk awhile and share a couple of beers. And then, the first thing you knew, it was one or two in the morning, and Anita would be winding up her show with a few rousing Texas songs. If she wasn't too tired, she'd invite Clint to a corner table where they had some privacy and could share conversation and a few drinks together. But nothing more. Anita belonged to no man and to every man. Clint figured to thaw her reserves and bed her down. That challenge alone was enough to keep him in San Antonio for the rest of the year if that was what it took to find out if Anita was as good at making love as she appeared to be. There were few women who had intrigued and aroused him as much as this one, and he was not a man who gave up easily. But so far, he hadn't even been able to get her alone in her room.

But in all honesty, Anita or not, Clint liked San Antonio, and if he had been a cowboy like most of them that passed through town at this time of year, he would have gone with the trail drives north to Abilene or Dodge City.

"Say, Clint," the bartender asked, "ready for another beer?"

"Nope."

The bartender nodded. "When you are, just holler."

Clint nodded. And right at that moment he saw Anita emerge from her room and stand on the balcony to survey the evening crowd. When she spotted Clint, she smiled and waved. Clint waved back. Anita was a fine-looking woman in her low-cut dress and her strawberry-blond hair piled up on the top of her head. She was wearing a black lace dress that fit her like a buckskin glove, and her face was pale and heart-shaped. Anita had long, shapely legs, a dazzling smile and summer-sky-blue eyes. Educated in an exclusive girls' school outside of Boston, daughter of a wealthy eastern attorney, Anita had fled from the rigid stricture of her up-bringing and arrived in Texas just after the Civil War.

She had worked several odd jobs and suffered a fair degree of harrassment from employers who wanted to get into her pants. Finally, she had come to the Alamo Saloon and demonstrated that she could sing. Dancing came easy, too, and before long, she was the saloon's main attraction. She had convinced the owners of the Alamo to hire a few more girls to join her in a chorus line. The girls who had auditioned were all prostitutes, and the three who had won the job had never been back to their cribs on the back streets. Four dancing and singing girls gave six shows, one every hour until quitting time. And for that, they were paid very well indeed.

"I don't know how you got so lucky as to be the one she obviously favors," a cowboy said as he watched Anita come down the stairs.

Clint shook his head. "Lucky at cards, lucky with women," he said. "They'll both run hot and cold through the course of a man's lifetime."

The cowboy hooted, "Well, when your luck runs cold with that particular woman, I sure wish you'd mention my name!"

Clint laughed as he started across the room to join Anita.

Suddenly a man shouted a hoarse cry of warning, and the bat-wing doors banged open. Hoyt stepped inside with a double-barreled shotgun balanced in his meaty fists. He was wild-looking and his face was contorted with rage. Clint realized that the man must have drunk his whiskey fast and then been standing just outside the saloon waiting for him to pass near the bat-wing doors where he would be an easy target.

The Gunsmith's hand streaked for the Colt on his hip as he dove for the floor. The shotgun boomed, and Clint felt a stab of pain at the blast, which cut into the floor and sent a shower of sawdust into the air. Men bellowed and women screamed. The Gunsmith hit the sawdust and fired at the same instant. The gun in his fist bucked, and he saw a red rose blossom right out of the center of Hoyt's chest. The crazed rancher staggered, tried to aim his shotgun at Clint and would have succeeded if the Gunsmith hadn't drilled him right between the eyes with a second bullet that came only a split second after the first.

Hoyt dropped the shotgun, and his mouth fell open as he covered his face and quickly backpeddled out the door. Clint heard his body hit the boardwalk, and he knew Hoyt was dead.

Thick white smoke hung in the room, and the first person to move was Anita, who raced down the stairs to throw herself at the Gunsmith's side and cradle his head. "Are you all right?"

"I was hit," he told her, "but if you aren't an angel, then this must not be heaven, and I guess I'm still alive."

Anita hugged his face to her wonderfully large and incredibly soft bosom. "Oh, Clint," she said, "if you're hurt, I'll . . ."

Clint struggled to pull his face from her bosom for she was smothering him in silk, lace, and flesh. "Take it easy, honey. I'm all right!"

A moment's inspection confirmed that assessment. A few pellets from the shotgun had caught the Gunsmith in his right buttock, but when Anita tried to unbuckle his gunbelt and then pull down his pants, Clint drew the line.

"It'll wait until I can get to the doctor's office," he said firmly, not wishing to endure the indignity of having his pants pulled down in front of a crowd.

"Then let's get you to a doctor at once."

"No," Clint said, making his voice sound weak and shaky. "I can't make it that far. I think I'd better be taken up to your room. Send a man to fetch the doctor to me."

He had spoken in a quiet voice meant only for Anita. But he had not spoken quietly enough. He had been overheard by the same cowboy who had admired Anita only minutes ago. The cowboy crowed like a rooster. "You boys hear that! The Gunsmith has just got himself all figured out a way to get up to Anita's room! Hell, someone shoot me in the ass, and I'll go along, too!"

Clint gave the big-mouthed cowboy a murderous look. But it didn't help. The entire room was already hooting with glee. Bunch of damned hyenas, Clint thought. They're just a bunch of jealous sonofabitches.

Chapter Two

"Live by the gun, die by the gun," the old doctor said as he used a pair of oversized tooth-pulling forceps to remove the shot from Clint's buttocks. "You were just damned lucky to get out of that alive. A man with a double-barreled shotgun ain't supposed to miss at close range."

"I know," Clint said through clenched teeth. "But I guess he was drunk and I had just enough warning."

The doctor seemed not to have heard. "Yessir, I seen a lot gunslicks like you come and go. They come, then they go to Boot Hill. You ought to hang up your six-gun and settle down peaceably. You're a gunsmith of some merit, I understand."

The doctor jammed the forceps in deep, and Clint dug his fingers into Anita's mattress. "Jesus," he whispered, "can't you use anything smaller than those damned old tooth-pullers!"

"Nope. You sure drilled Hoyt clean. Best shooting I ever saw. Got that worthless skunk right between the eyes. They say he backpeddled out the door, but he had to have been working on pure muscular reaction. He was dead the instant the bullet penetrated his brain. I was surprised he even got off a second shot the way you hit him in the chest. He was a horse, but no man can take two .44-caliber bullets the way that he did. Nice shooting."

Clint took a deep breath and mopped his brow. "How many more pieces of lead have you got left to remove?"

The doctor jammed the forceps deeper into his flesh, and Clint had to bite back a scream. A moment later, he heard the familiar ping of lead hitting a washpan. "That's the last of 'em. There may be one or two in real deep, in which case you can use 'em as a joke when people tell you to get the lead outa your ass."

The doctor chuckled at his own joke. Clint did not appreciate his style of humor. "If there was, what would happen? I mean, would they work themselves out, or would I have to have 'em removed later? If that's the case, I'd just as soon finish this right here and now."

"Ah," the doctor said, grunting as he stood up and wiped off his bloody forceps and surveryed his handiwork. "Don't be in such a hurry to endure more pain. Hell, you keep up the way you're doing, gambling and such, and you'll get shot to death anyway."

"Thanks," Clint said. "But I've been playing cards since I was twelve years old. My Pa taught me the finer points of dealing cards and throwing dice. What he didn't know, I picked up over the years in what I consider a very expensive, but worthwhile, education by some of the frontier's best gamblers. Now that I am skilled, I see no reason to quit."

"Suit yourself," the doctor said as he applied a bandage over the damaged flesh, then snapped his medical bag shut with finality. "But you're still young and you seem bright. Too bright to have the reputation as the fastest gunfighter in the West. You know that someone is always going to be trying to kill you, Gunsmith. Best thing you could do for yourself would be to go to the East, put on a suit, and change your name. Marry a respectable girl, have a family, and open a little shop."

Clint rolled over onto his good buttock and reached for

the bottle of whiskey that the doctor had provided for medicinal purposes. Clint took a long pull on the whiskey, and it helped to numb the pain. "You charge for advice as well as the doctoring?"

"I do not. The advice comes free."

"Well," Clint said, not liking a man who told other people how to spend their lives, "free is about what your advice is worth. You have a blacksmith's touch, Doc."

"You owe me ten dollars," the physician said gruffly. "And the next time I have to patch you up or pick pellets out of your ass, I'll double the charges."

"There won't be no next time," Clint promised. "And that's a fact."

The moment the doctor was gone, Clint laid his head down and rode the pain as if it were a bucking horse. Oh, he'd been in a lot worse shape, and there were no less than six bullet scars on his body and a few more caused by the knife. He'd been beaten over the head with pistols, whiskey bottles, and once even by an Apache war club, and he'd always managed to survive. But damned if this didn't hurt about as much as anything he'd suffered yet. Even worse was the indignity of the thing.

Down below in the saloon, he could hear Art beating on the piano, and Anita and her girls singing and dancing up a storm. Men were hooting and shouting, and it sounded like they were having a high old time. Clint took another drink, and the whiskey immediately began to take effect. Let the men down there have their fun. When the show ended, Anita was coming up here to her room, and he'd be waiting.

Clint smiled through the pain. He wasn't sure if any woman was worth getting shot in the ass for, but Anita was about the closest thing he had ever seen to being worth such a price. He looked around the room. It was small, but then, they always were. Nicely decorated though, and neat and clean like the woman herself. Lace curtains, knickknacks on the dressing room table, a few pictures that Clint could not see very clearly by candlelight, and a large wardrobe. The room even smelled like Anita, sort of like rose-petals.

Clint took another sip of whiskey and closed his eyes. He hoped she was a sympathetic woman, because he was going to milk this shotgun wound for all it was worth.

The Gunsmith woke to find the room still in darkness, save for a flickering bedside lamp. When he turned his head, he saw Anita sitting beside his bed with a coffeepot and two steaming cups.

"Thank goodness you finally woke up, Clint! I was starting to become very worried about you."

"What time is it?"

"Nine o'clock," she told him.

He did not understand. It had been eleven o'clock when the doctor had left the room.

Anita read his confusion. "Clint," she explained patiently, "you slept all last night and all of today."

He started to sit up, but the sharp pain in his backside brought back the sudden reminder of his circumstances. "Ouch!"

Anita's smile faded. "It must really hurt. That's why the doctor added an opiate to your whiskey. In fact, I think he added much too much. I was afraid you might never awaken."

Clint silently cussed the doctor, who had certainly gotten even. "I never slept over ten straight hours in my life," he said. "And I still feel groggy and half asleep."

She came over to his side and sat down primly on her bed. "The doctor told me that you were in a very foul mood last night. But I certainly understand."

He slipped his hand around her waist and tried to draw her closer, but she resisted. "I have to go," she said, "the girls are ready, and the music has begun."

Clint did hear Art and his piano again. "Hang the music," he said grumpily. "I need some comforting."

"I'll send someone up if you can't wait until I come off my shift."

"I gotta wait until two in the morning?"

"Of course. You may be convalescing, but I'm a working girl. I have a contract with management and an obligation to our customers."

Clint was not pleased. "Is it going to be worth the wait, or are we just going to hold hands and talk when you come in tonight?"

She laughed and stood up. She swayed over to her wardrobe and paused to consider which of her dresses to wear. A decision made, she simply untied the little sash at her waist and shrugged out of the pink wrapper. Clint sat up fast and sucked his breath into his mouth as he stared at her bare backside, which was magnificent. "Turn around. Please."

Anita turned. Clint's eyes bugged, and if he had been a well man he would have jumped the woman right on the spot. But he was not well, and before he could do anything she turned her back on him and dressed quickly. Heading for the door, she blew him a kiss.

"You're a man-killer," he said with a smile.

She stopped and turned back to regard him seductively. "No, I'm not, Clint."

"How can you say that to a man who has just seen what I've seen and then has to wait another six hours to enjoy this vision?"

Anita shrugged. "I just wanted to make sure you would be awake when I came in tonight. That's all."

"Oh, I'll be awake all right."

The door closed behind her, and Clint's eyes sparked with desire. With his mind still filled with the woman and her lush figure, he absently reached out for the bottle of whiskey at his bedside and took a long pull.

Suddenly, he remembered that the whiskey was laced with sleeping drugs. Clint broke out in a cold sweat and eased out of bed. He took a couple of steps, and then he felt as if his legs were turning to rubber. The opium and whatever else the damned doctor had laced the whiskey with was incredibly powerful. Clint lunged for the bed, and the moment his body flopped across it, he felt himself slipping back under.

If I miss out again tonight, he thought, I'll kill that goddam doctor. I'll just kill him for certain!

"Clint," she said, her breath warm in his ear, "wake up, darling."

He woke up slowly, feeling a nice sensation running over his body. Clint opened his eyes and saw that the room was bathed in soft lamplight. He was fully undressed except for the large bandage taped to his buttocks. Anita was also fully undressed and lying beside him. Her hands were massaging his manhood, and it was already far more awake than he was. His penis was long and stiff.

"You're beautiful," he said in a thick voice.

She sat up, her breasts proud and high. "Despite all the scars I've counted on you, you're not so bad yourself."

"I've been through a few wars in my lifetime."

"I'll make you forget all about them tonight."

Clint smiled. "Anytime you're ready."

She was ready. She slid down his body, her tongue making circles on his belly and then his hips and finally, the insides of his thighs. Clint moaned with anticipation, and when she took him into her mouth, it was hard and quick, the way a big-mouthed bass took bait. Clint reached down, and his fingers wound themselves in her long strawberry-blond hair. His buttocks ached, but he just knew it was worth the sacrifice. She was very, very good.

He would have liked to have rotated his hips, but when he tried, he felt the wound pain him so he lay still and allowed her to do all the things that she wanted. And when he could not stand it a moment longer, he panted, "Come up here!"

She was burning with her own desire. Her eyes flashed, and her lips were moist and full. He lowered his head to her breasts and when his mouth sucked gently on her hard nipples, she cooed with pleasure. "I want it quick," she breathed. "I haven't had a man in so long."

"That's your fault," he said. "Every man in San Antonio has been after you, lady."

She smiled. "I know. Aren't you the lucky one."

Clint could not argue with that at all. He rolled Anita over on her back and shoved her knees wide apart. She reached down and grabbed his pulsing penis and guided him into her slick, hot womanhood. She cried out with pleasure and arched her back. He drove himself in hard, and she raked his back with her fingernails. Clint began to slam his body in and out of her for she was the kind who liked it rough and ready. Later, he would use finesse and tantalize her until she begged for more. But right now, he felt his own passion building so fast that he could not contain himself.

"Oh yes!" she cried, her heels moving up and down on the sheets, faster and faster, exactly in time with his thrusts. "Oh . . . oh yes!"

She came like a volcano blowing off the top of a mountain. She began to buck and squeal, and her legs drummed up and down on the bed as his own body slammed into her and began to spew his seed far up inside of her hot wetness.

"Don't stop!" she moaned. "Don't ever stop."

Clint gritted his teeth and gave her all he had. He had no intention of stopping and, yes, this was definitely worth getting shot in the ass.

Chapter Three

Clint settled right into a highly enjoyable routine with Anita. Actually, the hours weren't that much different from the time he had spent before with her except that he now spent them in her bed. She was a wonderful playmate and, being bright and educated, Clint found that he enjoyed her mind almost as well as her body. Anita could quote Shakespeare, and sometimes recited love poems during the height of their passionate unions. This greatly excited the Gunsmith, and he had to be careful not to completely exhaust himself in her. More and more, he found that he yawned a lot in the evenings and stayed later and later in her bed until he was creeping out at sunrise.

They weren't fooling anyone in San Antonio that cared to notice—and a lot of people did take great interest in those sorts of things. Clint and Anita remained the hottest topic of conversation in the Alamo Saloon until the day that Richard Bates rode the stagecoach into town.

Clint happened to be standing next to his upstairs hotel room window when the stage rolled down the main street and pulled up at the station. As always, the stage attracted a fair amount of attention from the cowboys and old men who had little better to do with themselves. Sometimes there would be fresh women on board for the saloons or the cribs, a fact that was worth knowing. The cowboys figured that anything fresh was better than what they had been having for the last few months or years. Never mind that a "fresh" whore might have only traveled one hard day from her last job and that she wasn't fresh at all. She was new in San Antonio, and therefore, suddenly desirable. She could tell a customer about someplace he might not have been yet. About how another town or part of the country was different from this. Once, a pigeon-toed girl from Oregon had arrived and, for hours, the boys had argued whether such a girl would have webbed feet, being born and raised in such rainy country. That very same night, the first cowboy to pay her a visit settled the issue, and more than a few dollars passed hands when he declared she didn't have webbed any-thing.

But of all the women that had arrived in the past few years, none had stirred the hearts and imaginations of the men in San Antonio like Anita. Not only was she the freshest, prettiest single woman ever to arrive by stage unescorted, but she also had a slight Boston accent that curled the toes of the cowboys and made her seem so high-brow. When they discovered that she could read, write, and had actually graduated from a fancy girls' boarding and finishing school, the cowboys had treated her like a queen. The fact that she had taken only a few select lovers since and danced with hurdy-gurdy girls did not tarnish her nearly angelic image among the cowboys and working men who nightly flocked to the Alamo to see her perform.

But Richard Bates was another story altogether. At first glance, he seemed to be just another one of the many drum-mers or gamblers that came through town, stayed awhile, and then had to leave very suddenly or get planted in Boot Hill. But when Clint saw the tall, dapper young man, he knew that there was something special about Bates. Something that set him apart from the ordinary run-of-the-mill drifter and petty shyster.

He had bold good looks, a quick and dashing smile with lots of white teeth, and he was dressed in a tailored suit. When men passed, he spoke pleasantly, but without deference to any man. When women passed, no matter how old, ugly, or cross-looking, Richard Bates doffed his derby and bowed ever so slightly at the waist. With his long, wavy brown hair, his smile, and the deep cleft in his chin, he was so charming that almost every woman he met was dazzled.

Bates had an enormous crate that was unloaded from the boot of the stage, and his own trunk, which was large enough to carry Anita's entire wardrobe. But it was the crate that caused the most interest, and when the people of San Antonio saw how it took four strong men to carry it across the street to the hotel, their interest was heightened all the more.

No longer did the conversation buzz around Clint and Anita. Everyone wondered what the new dude in town was up to and what in tarnation it was that was so heavy in the wooden crate. Richard Bates seemed to be a man of complete mystery. He refused to reveal his business, saying only that he would announce his intentions as well as the content of the crate in good time.

Days passed, and the curiosity intensified until Bates proclaimed that he would unveil the contents of the crate in the town plaza on Sunday at noon. This caused a near fever-pitch of excitement. Most men figured the crate held little more of interest than some replacement parts for a wagon or a windmill. Other men speculated that there was a small but solid silver cannon in the crate, a cannon that had been found in the Gulf of Mexico waters and which had once belonged to the famous pirate, Jean Lafitte.

"What do you think there is in that crate?" Anita asked

Clint one night, right in the middle of their lovemaking.

Clint was annoyed that her mind should be on such a thing at a time of great passion, and he was unable to hide his anger. "Who gives a damn?"

Anita being wise and perceptive, gave herself completely to further the joys of intercourse and said no more until they were both satisfied, and Clint was pulling on his boots. "Well," she ventured, "I just wondered what you thought about it. I don't think there's anything to the cannon theory, do you?"

"Nope. If it were a cannon, it would take ten men to lift it," Clint said, for he had also been putting some thought to the matter. "I think it's just a box of hardware that he's selling."

"Hardware? What kind of hardware?"

"Oh, axes and hammers. Packages of nails and stuff like that."

Anita frowned. "I sure hope not. If that's all there is to it, folks are going to be mighty upset. They're expecting something pretty exciting on Sunday. Better not be any old common hardware. Not after all the mystery he's created."

Clint shrugged. He was sick to death of hearing about Bates. If he were still a sheriff, he'd demand that the man end all this nonsense and reveal the contents of the heavy crate and be done with it. Clint did not like surprises, and he figured that this one would be nothing but a mighty disappointment.

Sunday afternoon finally arrived and not only were most of the citizens of San Antonio present, but two large cowboy outfits had actually delayed their trail drive north for a couple of days because their cowboys threatened to quit rather than ride off before Richard Bates opened his damned old wooden crate. The crate was placed right smack in the center of the plaza, and everyone was allowed to touch it and place their bets.

Richard Bates remained calm and cool, but Clint could see that he was sweating and his outward calm was simply a façade.

The old mission bell at the Alamo struck twelve times, and Richard Bates raised his hands into the air and waved for silence. "Ladies and gentlemen," he began, using both terms very loosely, "I am aware of the excitement that has become focused around this crate. I am happy to tell you that your excitement is entirely justified. You will not be disappointed when I have this crate opened in a few moments."

A drunken cowboy yelled, "Then it is the goddam silver cannon. There goes twenty dollars shot to hell."

"Please," Richard Bates said. "The crate does not hide a silver cannon. What would be the point? No, what I have inside this crate is so revolutionary it will change the face of the West. It will tame and civilize this wild country, allow families to build and plant crops, and ranchers to no longer fear their herds will vanish in a blizzard as they drift, tails to the wind. No, what I am about to show you is nothing less than a miracle!"

He twisted around to signal three hired workmen who stood ready to act. "Open the crate!"

The workman had axes and they attacked the big crate like whiskey-crazed Indians hoping to find more firewater. The crate was bound up with rope, and when the ropes were severed, the sides of the crate dropped, and there stood a huge spool of wire unlike anything that had yet been seen by the Texans. It was double stranded and had thousands of mean-looking little barbs attached.

"Barbed wire is what it's called, my friends! It is lighter

than air, stronger than steel, and more effective in containing cattle or horses than any stockade ever built! It requires almost no room, exhausts no soil, shades no vegetation, makes no snowdrifts, and is both durable and cheap!"

When there was absolutely no reaction from the audience, Richard Bates grabbed a strand of wire and quickly raced around and around the spool twice. He stopped and held the uncoiled wire up in his fist. *"This* is the future of the West. Step right up and place your orders. I have here enough wire to fence only two thousand acres but there is more — boxcar loads more — on the way from Illinois where the demand is outstripping the known supply. So step right up and place your order!"

No one moved. A big cattleman named Enos Holt spat tobacco at Bates' feet. "Mister," he drawled meanly, "you got about as much sense as a rattlesnake in the sun. You get that goddam stuff the hell outa Texas before we string you up by the neck with it!"

Bates paled. "But you don't understand. This could be your salvation. No longer will you have to worry about people grabbing your land. All you have to do is to fence it off. Fence it all off!"

"Fence it off, huh! What in the hell kind of idiots do you think we are? If we fence off the range, we'll be cutting our own throats. We need the open range to move our cattle up the trail to the Kansas railheads. Cut off the range and the northern trails with this damned stuff, and we'd be committing suicide. Now get it and yourself out of Texas!"

A chorus of shouts went up all around, and cowboys as well as ranchers turned nasty. They started shoving Bates, and it looked to the Gunsmith as though they were about ready to explode.

"Why don't we take Mr. Holt's advice and string him up

with this goddam stuff," a cowboy shouted.

"Yeah!" cried dozens of angry men.

They grabbed Bates and though he fought, he was help-less. They snatched an axe from someone's hand and cut a twenty-foot length of barbed wire from the spool and made a noose. "Let's find us a tree!"

"You've got to help the poor fool!" Anita cried. "Clint, do something!"

The Gunsmith had been of the same mind. Just because Richard Bates was a fool was no reason why he ought to be hung with his own wire, or even a rope for that matter. He'd broken no law, injured no one.

Clint pulled his six-gun and fired two shots into the air. It had the desired effect. The cowboys froze, and when they saw it was the Gunsmith, they listened.

Clint said, "All right, you've all had your fun, but it's gone far enough."

"He deserves to hang for introducing such stuff!" a cow-boy shouted in anger.

Clint moved forward and carefully removed the wire noose from around Richard Bates' badly scratched and bloodied neck. "I think you came to the wrong town to sell your wire."

"Damn right he did!" the rancher who had fired up the crowd howled. "That stuff would never hold Texas longhorn cattle anyway."

"Mr. Holt, I don't suppose you'd care to bet on that!" Bates shouted.

Holt was a large, red-faced cattleman from south of town. He was said to be the biggest and most powerful man in this part of the country, and he was both outspoken and arrogant. Challenged in public, he had no choice but to accept the offer. "Hell, yes, I'll bet you!"

Bates was furious. He touched his neck, and when he saw the blood he shook his head. "All right! I and the manufacturing company I work for will take all bets—even money—that my wire can stop any herd of Texas longhorns you care to pen. You choose a hundred head of steer, bulls, cows—it don't matter. And you put them inside my barbed wire pen which I will construct right where I stand, and they will not be driven out of that pen. Do you understand what I'm saying, Mr. Holt?"

"I understand that you are a young fool who is about to lose all his money and that of his employer. I'll take five thousand dollars of your money, Bates. Put up or shut up!"

"I'll cover that bet." Bates glared at the angry crowd who had him and the Gunsmith circled. "Any of the rest of you want in on this bet, then let's get a paper and pencil and write your names and bets down. I'll cover every last one of you!"

The crowd surged forward to bet. Clint leaned in close to the angry young dandy. "This crowd will come up with another ten thousand dollars. You and the folks you work for had better be able to cover it."

"Don't worry," Bates said. "What I can't handle, my boss can. We stand behind barbed wire all the way. It will revolutionize ranching and farming and tame the West. Do yourself a favor, sir. Bet on my wire and reap certain fortune."

"No, thanks," Clint said, studying the wire and figuring such flimsy-looking stuff could never work, although he was impressed with the design of the two strands, which quite obviously kept the barbs from twisting or sliding. From Bates' neck, the Gunsmith could plainly see that the barbs were damned sharp. But sharp or not, they would not intimidate the longhorn, a beast who had cut its teeth on prickly pear and the sharp barbs of the Texas thickets.

Bates was taking bets as fast as they could be shoved in his direction. But he had heard Clint and had a moment to yell, "Suit yourself my friend and savior, but just don't bet against me!"

Clint shook his head and went to rejoin Anita who said, "Do you think he'll be all right?"

"Sure, until it comes time to cover all those bets. The Sunday excitement is all over here, and my tail is up to a buggy ride. How about it, girl?"

Anita beamed. "I know a place upriver where there's a nice swimming hole."

Clint smiled. "That sounds just right for us. Too bad I don't have any swimming suit, though."

She laughed and hugged his arm. "Yeah, me neither. Oh, well."

So they walked off the plaza at San Antonio and forgot all about Richard Bates until the day when it came time to pen the wildest longhorn cattle in all of Texas.

Chapter Four

If there had been an air of curiosity and high anticipation the week before Richard Bates revealed his giant spool of barbed wire, what took place the week after his challenge to Holt and the other cattlemen was absolute hysteria. No cattle herds were heading north to the Kansas railheads that week. No one talked of anything except Richard Bates and his crazy challenge to prove the worth of his ridiculous-looking barbed wire.

Every cowboy who could beg, borrow, or steal a few extra dollars bet against the brash Midwesterner with his new wire. On Monday, Bates had hired workmen to build a pen, and it was huge, big enough to hold a hundred Texas long-horn cattle. That surprised the ranchers and the cowboys, who had decided that Bates would probably do something underhanded like building the pen very, very small so that the longhorns could not get a good run at it. But Bates surprised them and instead of giving him credit for fair play, the cattlemen snickered and figured he was very, very stupid.

The Gunsmith was not so sure. He did not understand why the corral was three or four times as large as it needed to be, and finally, his curiosity got the better of him, and he went to see Bates and ask him straight out.

The young man was sitting in a café all alone. He was avoided by everyone, though cowboys did not go out of

27

their way to insult him as they had on Sunday.

"Well," Bates said, smiling but not able to hide the fact that life in San Antonio had not been much fun since his arrival. "You mean you're actually going to associate with a wild-eyed heretic like me?"

"Sure," Clint said, taking a seat. "I don't give a damn if you're popular or unpopular. You think you have something special, and you're trying to sell a bunch of it. What's the crime?"

Bates laughed. "I sure wish every man was as logical as yourself, Mr. Adams."

"Clint will do."

"Good," he said. "Call me Richard. So, you don't agree that I'm crazy?"

"Nope."

"And I haven't seen your name on the bet list so you aren't betting against me and the barbed wire, but neither are you betting on me. Are you a fence-straddler, Clint?"

The Gunsmith smiled. "I been called a lot of things, most of them bad. But never a fence-straddler. Nope. I just make it a habit to bet on things I know something about."

"Let me tell you something about this barbed wire, and you might decide that you can win big this Sunday," Richard said. "The stuff was invented by a man named Joseph Glidden. He was attending the De Kalb, Illinois, County Fair near my hometown when he happened to see an exhibit of a type of wood rail fence with sharp nail-like projections hammered along its length. Now, Mr. Glidden, he's a tinkering kind of man, and not long after he saw that fair exhibit he set out to improve the fencing. He hit upon adding barbs to wire."

"I saw the double strands," Clint said. "Pretty ingenious."

"You bet they are. The double strands are the key. You see, with just one strand, whenever a cow or horse rubbed up against the wire, he'd just slide all the barbs to one side and go on through. But with two strands and the barbs fixed by the twists, that can't happen. Also, the two strands keep the wire from sagging in the heat of summer and snapping in the cold. The twists give the wire the flexibility it needs. He invented, then patented, the wire I'm showng you and he called it, 'The Winner.' And it *is* a winner, Clint."

"Seems flimsy, and I find it hard to believe it'll stop a herd of longhorns."

Bates leaned forward and said in a low, confidential voice, "To be very honest with you, I'm not sure it can, either."

Clint blinked with surprise. "Then how can you take those bets?"

"What choice did I have? It was either put up or shut up." Bates sipped his coffee. "You of all people ought to understand why I had no choice but to take the bets. How many times have men challenged you to a gunfight? And how many times did you walk away?"

"Every chance I had," Clint answered.

"And if they gave you no choice but to crawl or stand?"

"Then I always stood and fought."

"Of course you did!" Bates cried. "And it's just the same with me. Holt gave me no choice but to back my words with cash or put my tail between my legs and slink out of Texas forever. I'm not any better at slinking off than you are, Clint. In fact, I'm sure we're both downright terrible at it. So I stood and I bet."

Clint sighed. "But you bet money you don't have. And you bet without knowing how good your wire is. It hasn't been tested under fire. Has it?"

"No," the young man admitted, "it has not. But I and Mr. Glidden believe in barbed wire. I came to Texas because, if I can win over these stubborn people, I can sell the rest of the country without any trouble at all. But if I lose here, that failure will dog me to the end of my days."

Clint looked deep into the man's eyes, and he saw no show or pretense. This was honest and Richard Bates really did believe that Texas would make or break his career. "Why'd you build such a large corral?"

Richard shrugged. "If the wire holds, I don't want people to say it was because the cattle couldn't get a fair run at it like they would on the range. This wire has to be tested successfully under range conditions or cattlemen and farmers won't buy it. So I'm having the workmen build a corral big enough to prove my claims without anyone saying I had an edge. Does that make sense to you?"

"It does." Clint frowned. "Let's just suppose that your revolutionary new barbed wire really works."

"It *will* work."

"Fine," Clint said. "I'm not a cattleman, but I do prize good horseflesh above almost everything but women."

Richard grinned. "Speaking of which, you've sure got the prize of San Antonio. If you ever . . ."

Clint raised his hand. "I've already got a list of men longer than my arm who are eager to take my place when I decide to leave San Antonio. What they don't realize is that Anita is a very headstrong woman. Nobody is going to put a brand on her unless she wants them to."

"I already figured that," he said. "And to be honest, if I lose this next Sunday and those longhorns do bust through my pen, not even you will be able to save me from a necktie party with my own barbed wire. But I sure appreciated what you did for me already."

"Let's get back to the question of horseflesh for a moment," Clint said. "It seems to me that your wire is going to cripple a lot of good animals. Animals are accustomed to fencing that they can easily see. Hell, this stuff of yours is so damned thin that horses will just run right into it and wind up being torn all to pieces."

"That's a sad truth, Clint. And one I can't argue with you about. In fact, I'd have to admit that we've already had that happen a few times back home, and the results were terrible. Horses, good horses, destroyed with wire cuts. It's something that Mr. Glidden and I both feel awful about, but you have to balance that against other things."

"Such as?"

"Such as small Midwest farmers who are sick and tired of having their crops trampled by cattle, buffalo, stray horses, and any drunk cowboy who comes riding through. We're talking about acres of corn, barley, and wheat that are being destroyed by stray livestock. Barbed wire is the *only* salvation for those people. There's not enough wood on the plains to build wood fences, there's not even rocks to build walls like they do in New England. There's nothing but our barbed wire. It's a godsend to the Midwestern farmers, and it will be the same to the farmers and ranchers in Texas."

Clint nodded. Sodbusters and small farmers did need protection. Crops were their livelihood, and Clint had seen those people nearly starve to death and lose their land after livestock had devastated their fields. It wasn't right, and they did deserve to be protected.

"Besides," Richard was saying. "I have my own theory about barbed wire. I believe that it will only take a generation or two for domesticated livestock to get used to the stuff and then they'll know better than to try and run through it as if it doesn't exist. You watch cattle and horses. They'll only hit my wire a few times and then they won't come near the stuff."

"If they're not already bleeding to death," Clint said tightly.

"Yes. Mr. Glidden talks about putting out new types of

wire with shorter, duller barbs. Barbs that are less apt to rip into hide and tear it."

"Maybe he could even have barbs that spin on wire like a spur rowel," Clint said.

Richard's eyes widened. "By God! You might have just hit on something! Can I send your suggestion to Mr. Glidden?"

"Hell, yes," Clint said, with a chuckle. "Though I'm sure that any man smart enough to come up with 'The Winner' has thought about such things already."

"Perhaps," Richard said, still excited by the concept. "But it won't hurt to pass your idea along."

"Do what you want with it," Clint said, feeling a little flattered that an inventor might actually use his idea.

Clint lowered his voice so that only Richard could hear his next words because they were words that had to be said. "I don't approve of fencing the range, and I damn sure don't approve of making bets that you can't pay. But I understand what you're doing and why. And in a way, I hope you win."

"If I do, would you like to become partners with me?"

"In what?"

"In selling barbed wire. We'll make a fortune together!"

Clint shook his head. "I'm not much at selling things."

"Well, I am," Richard said confidently. "And I'll need protection."

"Not interested."

Richard shrugged. "I didn't think you would be, but I wanted to ask and make sure. Maybe you'll change your mind after Sunday."

"Not likely. But good luck. You've given the cowboys of this town something to talk about instead of Anita and me. We're both appreciative of the fact."

Clint started to leave.

"Clint?"

He stopped.

Richard Bates grinned. "I'm going to win a fortune next week. You get a few extra dollars, take a chance. I've told you about barbed wire, so you can't claim you don't have an edge. Bet on barbed wire and win!"

Clint had to give credit where credit was due. This man was such an uninhibited optimist. And as the Gunsmith strolled across the plaza, he stopped to watch the posts going down. They were set about ten feet apart and they were railroad ties rather than normal fence posts. Set deep and solid in hard ground. Clint reckoned the posts would hold if the wire did.

Maybe, he thought as he passed on over to the Alamo Saloon, if I get lucky at cards again this week and do a little extra gunsmithing, I will bet on barbed wire. But not at even odds. Not when every cowboy and cattleman in San Antonio is willing to give at least five to one on the cattle.

Chapter Five

The card tables were slow in San Antonio all week long because every cowboy with a dollar in his pocket either spent it on girls, whiskey, or else bet it on the one hundred Texas longhorns that were being chosen to test the barbed wire fence.

Still not ready for the saddle, Clint rented a buggy and took Anita out on the range to where the cattle were being selected. "I understand that every cattleman hereabouts has been invited to send along their biggest, meanest longhorns," Clint said as they neared the cowboy camp.

"I don't see how Mr. Bates and his wire has any hope at all," Anita replied. "He'd better have a pile of money come Sunday. If not, he's as good as dead."

"He's aware of the fact," Clint said. He drove the buggy into the camp and was greeted by many of the cowboys who regularly frequented the Alamo.

"Did you come to see the biggest, the meanest hundred cattle in all of Texas?" a cowboy asked.

Clint reined in the horse. "That we did."

"Then drive right over yonder. That's them being held by the men. We're still a few short, but the finalists are being winnowed down to the last dozen or so. Jest don't get in among 'em or even get too close."

"That bad, huh?"

The cowboy nodded his head. He was a tall, skinny kid with big ears to rest his ten-gallon hat upon. "Them's the meanest critters in the world. Why, they're so damned mean they'd kill each other if we didn't stop 'em. Big sonofabitches, too! Some of 'em must weigh thirteen, even fourteen hundred pounds."

That *was* big, considering the average Texas cowpony only weighed between eight hundred fifty or nine hundred pounds. The Gunsmith's own black gelding, Duke, weighed just over a thousand, and he was considered to be a mighty big horse.

Clint drove the wagon right over to the cowboys where they could see the selected longhorns. "My God!" Clint said. "They're monsters!"

Anita nodded. The longhorns were savage-looking animals. Even as she watched, two, a brindle steer and a dun bull, started hooking each other with their long, dagger-like horns. They came together like train cars, ripping and thrusting. Suddenly, the dun got a horn into the brindle's belly and lifted the animal right off its back feet. Blood cascaded out of the gored steer's side, and it bawled in agony.

Anita looked away quickly as a pair of cowboys raced in and lassoed the dun to pull it away, but they were obviously far too late.

Enos Holt came spurring his horse into the herd. "Goddammit!" he raged, "That brindle has my brand on him!"

The two cowboys had their hands full with the dun who was jerking both their horses all over the ground. Holt swore again and yanked his carbine out from his saddle boot. Clint figured that the man was going to put the brindle out of its misery but he was in for a surprise. Holt gut-shot the dun. The animal groaned and went down. The two cowboys stared, first at the fallen dun, then at Holt.

The old cattleman shouted. "I told McKeever that that goddam bull was loco, and he should castrate him. Better

I shot the sonofabitch now than later after he killed more good steers."

"But you shot him in the guts," a cowboy said with a horrified expression on his face.

"Sure," Holt snarled, "exactly the same place he gored my steer."

Holt rode away leaving the pair of cowboys to decide what to do next. Without any discussion, they both pulled their own rifles and put the two fallen animals out of their misery. But it was clear they were appalled by Holt's cruelty. The dun bull might have been loco but just as likely he was acting according to his instincts. But then, maybe Holt had been doing the very same thing.

"I don't like that man," Anita whispered.

"I don't, either," Clint said. "He's mean and he's ruthless. If I was Richard Bates and I happened to win money from him this coming Sunday, I'd watch my back very carefully."

Anita watched as more cowboys were called in to rope and drag the dead carcasses off to be butchered. "I'm ready to go back," she said.

Clint nodded. The dust was very thick, and there were a lot of horseflies in the air. He was glad that he wasn't a cowboy.

The big day arrived bright and clear, though there had been a lightning storm the afternoon before. But the pen dried out quickly and everyone in San Antonio waited expectantly as the one hundred chosen longhorns were trailed into town. Clint and Anita could see the entire plaza from the window of her second-story room, and they nipped at a bottle of good tequila while a huge crowd filled the plaza in anticipation of the show. Most everyone, however, stayed either on horseback or atop a wagon. There seemed to be few that doubted that the wild Texas cattle would go through the wire like a sickle blade through dry winter grass. And, if they got scratched up a mite doing it, no intelligent human being wanted to be standing in their way when they came charging through the plaza.

"I should have bet fifty dollars on the longhorns," Anita said.

The Gunsmith smiled. "You still can."

"And go down there among all that," Anita said, pointing to the boisterous and very confident crowd that had begun cheering as the longhorns were driving into the plaza. "No, thanks."

Clint sipped his tequila and studied the pen. Richard Bates had strung four strands of his fancy new barbed wire as tight as guitar strings. Even from a distance, Clint could see the barbs gleaming wickedly in the sun. He could also see Bates himself, still taking bets that he could not cover. Still smiling and waving and acting like a candidate for some damned political office.

"What odds would you give me?" he asked the beautiful woman beside him.

"What do you mean?"

"I mean, if I wanted to take your bet."

"Are you serious? After what we saw out on the range you'd actually bet on the barbed wire?" Anita could not believe that he wasn't joking.

"I might."

She rolled her eyes up into her head as if he had gone crazy. "You name the odds and I'll take them. Rock walls couldn't hold those crazy cattle."

"Two to one," Clint said. "Your fifty dollars against my twenty-five."

"I don't need your charity," Anita said. "You know that."

"I know it all right. But for the sake of interest, do we have a bet?"

"Why sure!" Anita stuck her hand out and they shook. "But I have to tell you something, darling. You could have gotten at least five to one odds down there on the street. Hell, you could have gotten ten to one odds!"

"At least," the Gunsmith said in agreement. "But I never squeeze a lady."

"Not much you don't," Anita said with a knowing wink of her eye. "Oh, look! They're going inside now!"

Clint leaned forward to watch. The longhorn cattle were being hazed into the big wire pen. They looked out of sorts and were tossing their heads around. The cowboys were having a difficult time keeping them from breaking into the crowd. It was a tense moment.

But the cowboys did manage to get the cattle inside. Enos Holt himself along with several other cattlemen went into the pen with them. Almost immediately, Richard Bates had his own men wire the entrance shut.

"Well," Clint said. "The show is about to begin."

Anita appeared struck by guilt. "Clint, you really don't have to pay me if you lose. I think you've drunk too much tequila already."

Clint laughed outright. "The hell I have. I like the bet just fine, and if I win, I expect your fifty dollars to be in my hand."

Anita was dressed in her pink wrapper. She let it fall open a little so that Clint could see her lovely breasts. "If I lose, I'll put something in your hand, honey, but it won't be my fifty dollars."

The Gunsmith felt himself stiffen in his Levi's. If, by some miracle, Richard Bates actually did manage to contain the wild cattle below, the Gunsmith knew he would exact his winnings one way or the other.

"Here we go!"

There was little in the way of preliminaries. The hundred

chosen cattle were cantankerous, and they were more than eager to bolt for freedom. So when the cattlemen drew their six-guns and emptied them skyward, the wild longhorns sprang from a standstill and scattered like shot. What happened next was something never to be forgotten. The cattle hit the barbed wire from every angle and direction at once. Had they struck along one side only, their sheer weight would have brought the wire down, but as it happened, the tremendous force of their impact caused the thick posts to shudder and the wire to pop some of its heavy staples. But miraculously, it held!

Some of the longhorns tried to go between the strands and found themselves being cut terribly before they could back out. Other cattle hooked the wire with their great sweeping horns, but nothing happened except that the wire slipped down between their horns and deeply lacerated their polls. Those that hit the wire face- or chest-first suffered the most. They reeled back with blood streaming down their faces and legs.

The cattlemen were equally stunned as their longhorns. For a moment, they watched in total disbelief as the huge animals struggled to break through the cutting wire. When they failed, Enos Holt was the first to recover. He had a big rawhide quirt tied around his wrist and he went after the longhorns, slashing and driving them back into the fence. The other cattlemen followed suit. The longhorns charged the wire a second time, though anyone could see that they were reluctant.

Again, the wire ripped at them. Two poor animals became so tangled in the strands that they were immediately shot to death by cowboys so that they did not suffer.

Holt and his peers were incensed. Richard Bates was jumping up and down like a little kid rooting for his favorite baseball team. The crowd remained silent.

Holt and the other cattlemen again tried to drive the longhorns into the fencing. The second strand from the bottom had pulled loose and the cattlemen hoped that they had at last found a weakness to exploit in the fencing. They quirted and beat at their bloodied animals as the huge crowd watched hopefully, even desperately, for they had all bet on those torn, tragic cattle.

But the longhorns had had enough. They went right to the wire and when the first barbs bit into their faces, they bawled and retreated, and nothing, not quirts or slashing lariats or even gunfire could drive them forward again.

The last bullets were fired, the last hoarse curses thrown until the longhorns stood shaking with fear and dripping blood into the dust.

"My God!" Anita whispered. "I can't believe my own eyes!"

Clint expelled a deep breath, knowing that he had witnessed a dramatic event of great consequence.

Richard Bates threw back his head and howled with delight. Howled and danced and clapped his hands together. "Citizens of San Antonio, come and settle your bets! Mr. Holt, cattleman of Texas, I am ready to take your orders for barbed wire!"

Holt was not ready to give an inch. He rode his horse over to the wire and bellowed, "Cut this goddam wire and let me out of here!"

But Bates would have nothing of that. "No, sir!" he shouted. "You were the first to call me a fool and challenge my wire. And *you*, sir, should be the first to pay your debt!"

"I'll pay you, all right!"

Holt started to draw his gun. Clint was a good judge of character. He remembered how that man had gut-shot the dun bull without a moment's hesitation, and he knew what was coming as his own gun jumped into his fist. It was a long shot at a difficult angle, but he fired anyway and his bullet caught Enos Holt in the shoulder a fraction of a second before the Texan could kill Bates.

Holt tumbled from his horse. The longhorns spooked at the sight of a man on the ground and they shifted nervously. Two of Holt's cowboys just managed to drag their wounded boss through the wire before he was trampled or gored. But in doing so, they ripped their clothes to shreds and bloodied themselves.

Everyone looked up at the Gunsmith. "Better a bullet wound than to be hung for cold-blooded murder!" Clint shouted down at them.

No one could dispute that fact. But it was obvious from their faces that they were furious, and when Bates called again for them to pay him money owed, Clint knew that the young Midwestern wire salesman and promoter had made a lot of enemies.

Anita saw it, too, and summed up Clint's feeling when she said, "Someone will kill him for sure. He's as good as dead already."

Clint saw Bates grin and wave up to him to extend his thanks. "I can't let that happen," the Gunsmith said. "He's a brash young fool, but he's a bold gambler and I admire his courage and vision."

Anita frowned. "So what are you going to do about it?"

"Keep him alive, I guess."

"Oh, Clint! All you'll succeed in doing is earning yourself a bunch of his enemies. And probably, you'll get bushwhacked, and I'll lose you and then—"

Clint did not let her finish. He took her by the arm and pulled her back to the bed. "It's time to pay up," he said. "Fifty dollars'-worth."

Anita opened her pink wrapper and smiled as his lips found her breasts. "Have your way with me, Clint."

And he did. Fifty dollars'-worth.

Chapter Six

The banging on Anita's door brought Clint rolling off the woman to yell, "Whoever you are, go away!"

"I can't. It's me, Richard Bates. I've been shot."

Clint hopped out of bed. He snatched his six-gun from its holster, which was slung over the bedpost, but he did not bother to pull on his pants. When he opened the door, Richard was standing in the hallway with a big smile on his face.

Clint, stark-naked with only a gun in his fist, looked the man up and down and growled, "You said you were shot!"

"I lied," Richard admitted with a shrug of his shoulders. "I was shot at, but they missed. Can I come in?"

"Hell, no! But I ought to shoot you myself."

"Why not," Richard said, his grin slipping badly. "Everyone else in San Antonio is bound and determined to do it. If I'm going to die of lead poisoning, I'd rather it be administered by a professional like yourself than some rank amateur who might shoot me in the belly to die slowly."

"Clint, please," Anita said. "Why don't you let the poor man in?"

Richard glanced past Clint to see the woman in bed. She had pulled the sheets up to her chin and with her hair tossed and her face a little flushed from lovemaking, Anita looked ravishing.

43

"Thank you, ma'am," Richard said, not bothering to even glance at Clint but starting to step inside. Clint caught him by the shirtfront and brought the barbed wire drummer up short against the door-frame.

"*I* say who comes in and who doesn't. You wait outside until we're dressed and then I'll let you in."

Richard must have seen no percentage in arguing with an irritated man standing naked in the hallway with a Colt revolver clenched in his fist. Especially when that man had a reputation as someone who should not be crossed.

"Yes, sir," he said, backing across the hall. "But I wasn't kidding when I said I was on every cattleman and cowboy's wanted list. You're going to feel real guilty if they come charging up here and kill me before you and your beautiful lady can get dressed."

"It's a guilt we can live with," Clint said, slamming the door in his face.

"You were pretty hard on him," Anita said, hopping out of bed and reaching for her underclothes.

"He's a little too cocky for his own good," Clint said. "But underneath that brashness, I think he's worried."

"He ought to be and so should you," Anita said. "Enos Holt is not going to let either of you forget what happened down there today. You'd have been better off if you'd killed the man outright instead of merely wounding him."

"I don't work that way," Clint said. He dressed quickly. It was clear that Richard Bates was now a very rich but very hated man in San Antonio. The best thing for him to do would be to just pack up his big spool of barbed wire and get the hell out of this town while he was still in one piece. "You ready?"

Anita was fully dressed. She still looked flushed and a little excited, but at least she was respectable and so the Gunsmith walked over to the door and opened it. The only thing in the hallway was Richard Bates' derby hat.

"He's gone!"

Anita came running out. "Why did he go away?"

Clint picked up the hat. The crown was smashed in and when he turned the derby hat over, he saw fresh blood on the inside of the lining. "He didn't leave because he wanted to leave," Clint said tightly. "I'm afraid he left because he had no choice."

"But wouldn't he have yelled or . . . or something?"

That was exactly the question on Clint's mind as well. There was only one possible way that someone could have gotten behind Bates and stunned him before he had a chance to yelp a warning. Clint stepped over to the door opposite Anita's. "Who's room is this?"

"No one lives in it full-time. It's a room used strictly for . . . you know."

Clint knew. It was a room used just for the girls who worked the men at the Alamo. Clint placed his hand on the doorknob and drew his gun. He shoved the door open very suddenly. The room was tiny. Nothing more than a bed and a washstand. There were old, faded curtains on the windows but nothing hanging on the walls. The only piece of furniture besides the bed and the washstand was a broken hatrack. Other than those things, just a very naked and very dead woman.

Anita pushed in behind him and stifled a cry. "It's Lucy! Oh, my God!''

Clint let her by, and she hurried to the dead woman's side. The woman had been stabbed three times in the chest. Her plumpish body was lying sprawled across the bed, and her eyes were open and staring at the peeling paint on the ceiling. Anita sat down beside Lucy and touched her powdered cheek. "She was a nice person. A little crazy when she drank, but nice anyway."

Clint glanced quickly around the room. "Whoever knocked Richard Bates out must have known he would come here seeking my help. They used this poor woman as an excuse to get into this room. When I refused to let Bates in, they simply knocked him out and took him away."

"I wonder if they got all that money he won?" Anita asked.

"Somehow, I don't think so. If they had, they'd have killed him outright."

"But where could he have taken it? The bank is closed on Sunday."

"I don't know," Clint said. "There are a lot of questions to be asked. All I'm sure of is that I should have let the man in when he came to our door."

Anita nodded. "You told him that, if he was killed, it was a guilt we could live with."

"I wasn't being serious."

Anita looked up at him. "Maybe you weren't," she said, looking back at the dead prostitute, "but whoever did this sure was."

Clint headed for the door. Maybe someone down in the Alamo could give him the name of whoever had come upstairs with poor Lucy. That would be a start. Something to go on.

But downstairs, Clint struck out. He asked everyone who was sober enough to recall seeing Lucy earlier who she had gone up to her room with. The piano player summed it up when he said, "Hell, Lucy must go up and down those stairs with ten, fifteen guys every night. She was always busy. So busy nobody took much notice of who was going up with her when."

"I remember one fella she took up earlier," a girl who worked with Lucy said. "He was a big fella. Probably hung like a bull. He had red hair and the palest blue eyes you ever seen."

Clint was interested. "You ever see him before?"

"No. But he seemed to know his way around. He went right to Lucy and the next thing I know, they were gone. Might have been him. But then again, I was up and down those stairs a half dozen times myself this evening. A girl has to pay attention to the man that's paying her. Right?"

Clint didn't answer. He walked outside for some fresh air. Then he strolled down the street to the livery where he boarded Duke. The little office where the owner, a nice old fella named Bert, lived and worked was dark, so Clint knew that the man was already in bed and probably asleep.

The Gunsmith tiptoed into the barn and lit a match. He walked quickly down the row of stalls until he came to Duke. The big gelding nickered a welcome, and the Gunsmith reached into his shirt pocket and brought out a cube of sugar. He gave it to the black gelding and the animal's powerful teeth crunched, then he swallowed it. Duke nuzzled him for more sugar, but Clint scratched his ears instead.

"I sort of messed things up real bad tonight," he told the horse. They had been on so many lonesome trails together that Clint liked to talk to his horse. Duke was the best listener he had ever found. "Because I messed up, a woman is dead and Richard Bates might be as well. I sure wish I could do things over again. I'm afraid that sometimes, my brains slip down between my legs, Duke. I should have stayed with Bates until the cowboys and cattlemen sort of cooled off. But I went to bed with Anita, instead, and now everything is all messed up."

Duke nuzzled him affectionately. The gelding seemed to understand. And even though he could offer no advice, Clint felt comforted by the animal's quiet, solid presence.

Before he left, he dug out one more cube of sugar and said, "I think I'll go pay a visit to that Enos Holt fella. Of all the men I saw down in the plaza, he's number one on my list who'd want to kill Richard Bates."

With that decision in mind, Clint lit another match and let it show him the way out of the barn. Now that he had a definite plan of investigation, he felt better. It was funny, but sometimes talking to a good horse made good horse sense.

Chapter Seven

The desk clerk at the Stockman's House was very nervous when Clint asked for the room number of Enos Holt.

"Is Mr. Holt expecting you, sir?"

"He might be," Clint said.

The clerk, a thin, nervous man with oily black hair and a waxed mustache, swallowed and said, "I'm afraid you had better come back and try tomorrow. You must know that Mr. Holt was shot today."

"Sure I know," Clint said, "I'm the one that shot him!"

The clerk's eyes bugged, and he opened and closed his mouth a few times without saying a word. Clint resisted a strong temptation to reach across the hotel desk, grab him by the shirtfront and jerk him up on his toes.

"Mr. Adams, I really . . . really must ask you to leave!" the clerk finally managed to stammer.

Clint edged around the sign-in desk and moved up to the clerk. "I already shot my man for today, but I sometimes double up. You interested in living any longer?"

The clerk's thin lips moved silently and his pointy little chin began to bob up and down.

"Good," Clint said. "Room number?"

"Two-oh-four."

Clint brushed a piece of lint from the man's black frock

coat. "Thank you," he said as if he meant it with all his heart. "How many men are with Mr. Holt right now?"

"I . . . I . . ."

Clint grabbed the man by the nose between the big joint of his two middle fingers and twisted. "About how many?" he said gently.

"Four!" the clerk cried, though with his nose bent out of shape the word sounded like "fur."

Clint smiled and stepped back. He headed for the stairway and climbed slowly. The clerk was in a state of agitation and came running out into the lobby. "Please don't shoot up the room! It's our finest."

"Wouldn't think of it," Clint assured the man. "Now go back and hide behind your desk like a nice little hotel clerk."

The man obeyed. Clint reached the top of the stairs and walked down the plush hallway until he came to Room 204. He hesitated, then pressed his ear to the door. But this was a quality hotel and the doors were solid oak, and he could not distinguish the words being spoken inside. He was already on Holt's shit list, and so there was not much left to lose by busting down the man's door and raising some hackles. With that in mind, Clint stepped back and gave the door a powerful kick.

But the lock and hinges held! Suddenly, from inside, there was a shout. "Who's out there!"

The Gunsmith cussed at himself. He'd lost the element of surprise and there were four men inside. He'd bet about anything that at least a few of them were gunfighters. To go inside now would be like walking into a lion's den with a willow switch. It wouldn't be smart or healthy.

Clint backed down the hallway and then went down the stairs. When he reached the main floor, he turned on his heel. "If they ask who came calling, just tell them the truth and that I want to see Mr. Holt tomorrow. Tell them it's important."

Clint went outside and crossed the street. He stepped into the shadows between two buildings where he could see directly through the front lobby windows of the Stockman's House. It was not ten seconds later that he saw three men come bounding down the stairs, guns in their fists. One of them was very big with very red hair.

They turned to the hotel clerk, and Clint saw the desk clerk cringe like a mouse. It did not take a lot of imagination to know that they were shouting at him and demanding to know who had been up to Holt's room and then had tried to bust down the door. The big redheaded fella grabbed the clerk and shook him hard. He backhanded the clerk twice and even from across the street, Clint could almost feel how hard the blows were delivered.

"You don't have to rough up the mouse," Clint said. "But I'll guarantee you one thing, Red, when I meet up with you later, you're going to have to answer some tough questions."

The big man dropped the clerk. He had obviously told them their visitor was the Gunsmith, who would see Holt tomorrow. The four men made a big show of going to the front door of the hotel, guns still clenched in their fists, and looking up and down the street. Satisfied that they had accomplished at least something for their pay, they turned around and tromped back up the stairs.

Clint remained where he was for a while. Identifying the big redheaded man made him even more certain that Holt was behind the abduction of poor Richard Bates. The only question now was if Bates was alive or dead. If he was dead, the game was going to be slow and difficult because they'd have found his money. But if Bates was alive and had not talked, then there was still hope.

Clint edged out of the shadows. He headed for his own hotel room, not wanting to draw Anita into any kind of gun trouble. One way or another, tomorrow was going to be an interesting day.

They did not wait for him to come. Sometime around four in the morning as Clint was just crawling into bed, he heard footsteps approaching down the hallway. The footsteps halted just outside of Clint's door. The Gunsmith rolled off his bed and hit the floor with his six-gun ready. The bed was between himself and the door and he stayed low, ready for whoever might be outside to come rushing in to meet their maker.

But instead of the door bursting open, a note was slipped under it and the footsteps quickly moved away. Clint got up and went to retrieve the note. He lit a candle beside his bed and read the message.

The message was brief and Clint read it aloud. *"Better come to visit your woman pronto and before she's all used up."*

Clint's blood turned to ice water. Anita had a double lock on her door, but it had not kept someone out of her room. The Gunsmith grabbed his pants and boots. He buckled on his gunbelt and snatched up his shirt, not bothering with his hat. He slipped out of his room and headed down the stairs taking them silently, two at a time. When he reached the street, he jumped sideways, fully expecting ambushers to be waiting to gun him down.

But the street was empty. Quiet. Even the drunks and the rowdy cowboys had packed it in for the night. Clint hurried down to the Alamo. It never closed, though there were only a few men at the bar, and all but one of the poker games were over at this hour.

"There's trouble up there!" the bartender hissed as Clint moved swiftly toward the staircase.

"How many?"

"Three. They've been with Anita almost an hour. One of the girls said she heard Anita moaning."

Clint jerked his gun out of his holster and attacked the stairs three at a time. When he reached her door, he saw that it was bolted from the inside but that it had been jimmied open. There were splinters of wood on the hallway carpet. Clint debated whether or not to bust in shooting or knock, and when they let him inside, then shoot. He decided that he could not afford to take a chance that a stray bullet would hit and kill Anita.

He tapped the barrel of his six-gun on the door three times.

"That you, Gunsmith?"

"Yeah," he managed to say.

"Hang on just a minute. I want to surprise you."

Clint took a deep breath and let it out slowly. He knew that, once the door opened, some people were going to die if Anita had been harmed, and maybe even if she hadn't been harmed.

The bolt slid noisily and a voice said, "Push it open real slow and come in with your hands over your head."

Clint raised his hands. There was no choice. He pushed the door open and stepped into the room.

"Clint, please, help me!" Anita moaned, looking up at him with desperation in her eyes. There was a nasty bruise on one cheek and her lower lip was split and bleeding. Clearly, she had been roughed up pretty bad. She was bent over her own bed, naked, her legs spread wide apart. The big redheaded man was standing just behind her with his stiff penis in one hand and a six-gun in the other. The gun was pressed to the back of Anita's head. He was facing

Clint, his eyes glassy with anticipated pleasure as his powerful body poised ready to enter Anita from behind.

"Make one move and I'll blow her brains out and wouldn't that be a waste. I thought you'd like to watch the show. As you can plainly see, me and the boys got her all ready to have some fun."

Clint almost lost control as a wild rage to kill the red-haired man shook him to the core. He trembled and started to lower his hands, but two men were standing on either side of the door with guns in their fists. Their eyes were also bright with lust and kept darting at Anita.

Clint did the only thing he could do. Instead of moving forward in some vain and suicidal attempt to reach Anita as expected, he jumped straight back out the doorway into the hall so that the two men could not see him. The Gunsmith's hand streaked for his own weapon, and it came up just as the redheaded man swung his weapon at the door. Clint shot him where he stood. His big body jerked, and Clint drilled him again through the chest, and he bellowed like a wounded bull, then went reeling backward to crash through Anita's window and disappear in a shower of glass.

Clint jumped back to the doorway, shoved his gun around the corner in one direction and unleashed two bullets he hoped would find their mark. Then he turned the barrel of his gun and fired two more. He heard a body fall. Anita screamed and rolled off the bed to take cover. Clint had one bullet left and when a badly wounded man staggered into the middle of the room and tried to return fire, Clint shot him right through the forehead.

"Oh, Clint!" Anita cried, throwing herself across the room and burying her face against his shoulder. "It was terrible!"

"It's over," he told her. "They're all dead."

She was trembling so violently that he knew he could not leave her, and they sure could not stay in this room. Clint found her pink wrapper and pulled it around her. He picked her up and carried her outside, then down into the bar where the few customers who were still at the bar suddenly looked very sober.

"She's checking out for a while," Clint told the bartender. "You can tell the boss that she's going on a little vacation until this is all over."

The man nodded. "I hope you killed them all."

"I did," Clint said, as he carried the woman out of the Alamo Saloon and into the night. "I sure as hell did."

Clint knew he had made a big mistake in leaving Anita alone and unprotected. He had thought they would come for him and leave his woman alone. But he should have known that they were totally ruthless bastards who would play by no man's rules. The best thing he could do was to sneak Anita on the stagecoach heading for Austin. He could meet the stage a few miles outside of the San Antonio limits and then no one would know where she had gone.

It seemed like a good plan. But then, everything that he had done so far had been wrong. Pretty soon, he was either going to have to kill Holt and whoever else was behind this whole mess, or they were going to kill him. It was just that simple.

Chapter Eight

They were standing on the road, waiting for the morning stage. It was going to be a beautiful day, bright and cool. Clint had gotten Anita out of town hidden under a tarp on the floor of a buggy. Just moments earlier, sunrise had burst from the east to flood the country with a palette full of colors, but Clint and Anita scarcely noticed.

"Clint, please," Anita whispered. "Why don't you come to Austin with me. You know that Richard Bates is dead. There's nothing but trouble for you back in San Antonio."

But the Gunsmith shook his head. "I have a feeling that Bates is still alive."

"But why?"

"Because he's too smart to have let himself be taken with all the money he won yesterday. Anyone with any brains would realize that they had to hide that money quickly until it could be deposited in the bank or taken out of San Antonio entirely. And Richard Bates had his share of brains. No, I think he's still alive, and the reason for the trouble we've had is that Bates either can't, or won't, talk."

"You seem very sure of that theory."

"After you've been a lawman for a while, you sort of get hunches that generally prove correct. Why else would they come after me—through you—like they did last night? I was about the only man that believed in Bates. We weren't

57

friends, but I think he trusted me. In fact, I *know* he did. He even offered me a job."

"Doing what?"

"Protecting him in Texas while he sold barbed wire. He knew that the big ranchers would try to kill him. That's why he approached me, hoping my gun would save his life."

Anita shook her head. "I'm just afraid that, if I get on that stage, I'll never see you again. I'll always wonder what happened."

"I'll come to Austin to pay you a visit," he promised. "And if I never show, then you'll know for certain that I was killed. No one lives forever, Anita. And I'm not the kind of man who would grow old and take a rocking chair with good grace."

He had said it with a smile, and now, she brightened a little. "I'll never stop loving you for what you did for me last night. I've had my fair share of exciting men. I'll admit to that. But never one I didn't choose."

"Here comes the stage," Clint said. "Now, I want you to promise me you'll stay away from San Antonio until I come to Austin and tell you everything is safe. I'm going to have enough trouble just worrying about my own hide and trying to find Bates, without also worrying about you. Have we got a deal?"

She said, "Have I any choice?"

"No."

"Then we do have a deal, Clint."

The stagecoach was coming fast, and Clint walked out into the road and flagged it down. He and Anita embraced, not giving a damn that all the passengers and the driver were gawking. Clint had made sure that Anita had plenty of money to get a fresh start. Now, he paid the driver and helped his woman up into the coach.

"I'll be seeing you before long," he said.

"You'd better."

The door closed, and when Clint stepped back from the coach, the driver applied his whip, and the coach rocked forward and then gathered speed. Clint stood in the road a long time, so long that the coach disappeared entirely leaving in its wake only a faint rooster-tail of dust on the horizon.

When the Gunsmith climbed back into the buggy, he felt sad to see Anita go, but also as if a heavy weight had been lifted from his shoulders. Enos Holt and his powerful friends had proven themselves less than gentlemen when they had sent the redheaded man and those two other gunmen to Anita's room. Clint did not know if Anita had been raped, or if they had waited for him to come and watch so that he might be driven to confess where Bates had hid his winnings.

Either way, it changed nothing. Three men were dead, and the Gunsmith had some dirty work left to do in order ιo get to the bottom of the mysterious disappearance of Richard Bates.

Clint turned the buggy back toward San Antonio. About two miles to the east he could see a herd of Texas longhorns as they started the long drive up into Kansas. Clint could not help wondering if Glidden's new barbed wire invention, The Winner, actually would close off the cattle trails. He supposed it might, but not until after the turn of the century. Besides, there was talk of a new railroad line being built west out of New Orleans, and even a Southern Pacific Railroad linking San Antonio with Tucson, Fort Yuma, and Los Angeles. The Kansas Pacific Railroad was reaching for Salina, and it looked as if it would go all the way to Denver. Hell, Clint thought, even if the long trails do eventually get fenced off, by then, the West will have become civilized anyway. They'll ship all the cattle by rail and the poor old cowboy will never get to enjoy eighteen-hour days in the saddle. Or freezing nights, blistering sun, dust, hailstorms, or stampedes. Or even poison water, no sleep, dirt in his food, and scorpions in his bedroll.

The way Clint had it figured, there were some men who loved progress. Mostly young, ambitious fellas like Richard Bates. Men out to make their fortunes off change. Then, there were men like himself. Clint liked progress. He appreciated the fact that he no longer had to risk his life using those old unreliable cap and ball revolvers. The damned nipples had often fallen off or misfired. The black powder was often of inferior quality. Sometimes, the powder got wet and did not fire, or else it was too powerful and burst the gun apart in a man's fist, taking most or all of his fingers. Hell, in those days, if your old percussion .36-caliber Navy or .44-caliber Army actually fired six shots, it was a miracle. The black powder would also cause the firing mechanisms to foul and jam. Nope, Clint liked the new metallic cartridges just fine. Weapons as well as the standard of living were improving all the time. Clint didn't mind progress one damned bit. Progress was traveling from Omaha to Sacramento in the luxury coach of the transcontinental railroad, sipping champagne and remembering how, less than twenty-five years earlier, men, women, and even little children had suffered and died struggling across alkali deserts, freezing in the mountains and fearing an attack by Indians every bitter mile.

But there was a third kind of individual: those that hated progress. Any kind of progress. There were still mountain men alive and living in the past long, long after they'd stripped the rivers of beaver. Embittered and hating civilization, they'd gone wild up in the Rockies and were little better than animals themselves, relics of another time. Buffalo hunters were another breed on their way out. Ever since the railroad had linked the East with the West less than a decade ago, the great buffalo herds had been in a rapid decline. The buffalo hunters had slaughtered millions of the bison, selling their hides and leaving their carcasses to rot while the Indians starved. After the buffalo were gone, there came the bone-pickers and so it went, on and on. Every time a man lost his way of life, it was almost sure that he suddenly hated progress.

Hell, Clint thought, you either rode progress, or it rode you into the grave or an early retirement. The gunfighter days were almost at an end. Clint could see his own way of life as a frontier lawman disappearing. Wild Bill Hickok had been a shoot-first kind of man who had killed more than a few innocents. His kind, along with the old-time stagecoach robbers and outlaws, were doomed. Clint figured the good old days of law and order were about over. A sheriff almost had to explain to an outlaw what he was going to do next or some damned attorney would get the guilty man off on a legal technicality. Pistol-whipping drunks was out of favor, and God help the poor lawman who shot an innocent citizen because of an honest mistake. Maybe that was one of the reasons Clint had quit sheriffing and decided to spend his days either gunsmithing or gambling. Men would always need working firearms, and the urge to gamble was as instinctual as the urge to physically couple with a woman.

These were Clint's thoughts as he drove back to San Antonio and returned his rented buggy to the liveryman.

"Funny time for a ride in the country," the man said.

"I like to watch the sunrise out on the plains," Clint said. "Civilization sort of spoils it, don't you think?"

But the liveryman just shrugged his shoulders and continued cleaning stalls. "Hell," he muttered, "I'd just as soon sleep in every morning. If I never saw a sunrise again in my whole damned life it would be too soon. Besides, it's a whole lot safer to be asleep in bed at night. Did you hear all the ruckus last night?"

"Ruckus?"

"Sure. Hell, it sounded like a Civil War battle going on right here in town. I woke up and heard all kinds of shooting. Then this morning, when I got up I seen a man layin' in the middle of the street with glass all over him. He looked like he'd gone through an upstairs window."

"Well, I'll be."

"Don't you spend a lot of time at the Alamo Saloon?"

"I do."

"Well, that's where this fella was killed and throwed out of! And then, a little while later, I saw two more bodies being taken out of the saloon and on down to the undertaker's. I sure don't know why you didn't hear all that commotion."

"I guess I musta already been out on the buggy ride."

"I guess so," the liveryman said, though he sounded skeptical. "But like I said, a man is safest at night in bed."

"I couldn't agree more," Clint said. "But men are going to be men and prowl like cats at night."

"Not this man. I got a wife. She works over at the dressmaker's, and I feel real good staying home."

Clint clapped the man on the shoulder. "It's good to hear you say that. Honest work will keep a man from the temptation of the devil."

"Amen, brother!" the man said as he started pitching horseshit out of the stalls.

Clint grinned. He was talking nonsense. Hard physical work, especially if it was routine and monotonous, just made a man old before his time. The Gunsmith fed Duke another cube of sugar and then headed outside.

He was going to have some breakfast. A good big one. And then, he was going to see Enos Holt, and nothing would stop him this time.

Richard Bates, if he really were still alive, would be weakening. Time was running short.

Chapter Nine

Clint had started to head for a café for breakfast, but once out in the street, he had a change of heart. Enos Holt had to eat, and no doubt the man would eat where he stayed, at the Stockman's House. There was reported to be a fine restaurant there, and Clint figured he'd take a chance on catching the cattleman by surprise.

The dining room was still fairly empty when Clint arrived, because it was only six-thirty in the morning. He removed his hat and was met by a waiter. "Has Mr. Holt been down for breakfast yet?"

The waiter looked at Clint with a disapproving eye. The Gunsmith was dusty and unshaven. "Are you a friend of his?"

"An acquaintance," Clint said.

"Mr. Holt usually comes down at seven. But unless you have business . . ."

"I'll have a table and a menu," Clint said brusquely.

It was clear that the waiter was not pleased. The early patrons, Clint observed, were very prominent-looking. And as Clint was led toward a table, he wondered if he had enough money left to pay for his breakfast. No matter, if Holt came down with his gunmen, Clint figured he would probably not have time to finish his breakfast anyway.

"Whoa up, there!" he said, when the waiter stopped.

"Is something wrong?"

"Yes," Clint told the man. "Where will Mr. Holt be seated?"

"Over there," the man said, pointing.

"Fine, I want that table over by the wall."

"But that . . ."

Clint did not wait to hear the objection. No doubt he had chosen some other wealthy fella's special breakfast table. To hell with it. There was no brand on any of the tablecloths. He'd choose any table that was empty, and they could all lump it. It was just amazing to Clint how some folks got upset over such small things as having their own little routines disrupted. That was one thing about being a lawman, you never knew from one morning to the next what a given day would bring.

The waiter was clearly upset, but when Clint slammed his dusty Stetson down on the clean linen tablecloth, the man positively turned purple in the face. "I believe I should ask you to leave!" he hissed.

Clint reached down and picked up a tall glass of water. He raised it to his lips, took a sip and said, "Water is water no matter how fancy the glass. Ever notice that?"

"No, but you—"

Clint dumped it on the waiter's chest. The man was wearing a starched white shirt, tie, and black coat. When the water poured down his shirt and showered his polished shoes, he began to tremble with rage.

"Sorry," Clint said. "But if I were you, I'd just go ahead and scream. Cuss me out if it will help you feel better. Hell, all these fancy customers of yours sure won't mind. Go ahead."

The waiter turned and bolted. Clint sat down and, in a few minutes, placed his order. He was having fresh cantaloupe, sausage, Belgian waffles, a choice beef steak, and orange juice, in addition to his coffee. He figured, as long as he couldn't pay for anything, he might as well order as much as he wanted. They'd raise hell over a dollar as much as ten dollars.

While he waited, he checked his six-gun just to make sure that it was in good working order. He noticed that his inspection made some of the diners appear nervous, and they seemed quite shocked that he would clean the gun with his napkin, but what the hell. Clint had just been forced to kill three men, one of whom was preparing to rape his woman. He was tired, gritty-eyed, and not in the best of sorts.

His breakfasat came very quickly. Amazingly fast. Clint suspected that he had appropriated someone else's steak because they wanted him to eat and run without any more fuss or commotion. Well, the Gunsmith thought, as he went after the waffles and the steak, they might get a whole lot more than they bargained for when Enos Holt and his cronies arrived.

Clint was ravenous. He actually forgot about Holt until he had finished his breakfast and leaned back to sip his coffee. Fortunately, it had not mattered. Holt and several other prominent-looking cattlemen appeared at exactly the right time. They were talking loudly. Holt had his left arm in a sling and from the bulge of his shoulder, it was clear his wound was heavily bandaged. None of the cattlemen noticed the Gunsmith, who sat back against the wall, watching them with more than ordinary interest. These men were clearly in that third category, the ones who hated progress.

They had probably come into this country and fought both the Kiowa and the Comanche to carve a piece of Texas for their own. They had started driving herds north shortly after the Civil War, when the wild cimarrones were more plentiful than prairie dogs and worth just about as much. Now, they were powerful and wealthy, and they wanted to maintain things exactly as they were. The last thing in the world they wanted was barbed wire stretching across the cattle trails.

Clint finished his coffee, and when the check arrived, he smiled, picked it up, and said, "This excellent meal is going to be on Mr. Holt. Present the check to him, please."

The new waiter did not care who paid it. He simply shrugged and walked over to Enos Holt, who had taken his seat and was ordering. He bent at the waist and gave the check to the man, and Clint saw him pointing his way as he explained.

When Holt saw the Gunsmith, he stiffened. He grabbed the check, wadded it into a ball, and hurled it at the floor.

"Thanks!" Clint called, standing up as the cattleman tried to figure out what to do.

Clint walked over to Holt. "I think I know what you want from me, and I know what I want from you. So why don't we have a peaceable little conversation?"

"You shot me, you sonofabitch!"

Clint backhanded the man hard enough to rock him in his chair. He broke Holt's lip and it bled. Before the ruthless old man could erupt, Clint had his six-gun out and was sticking it right in Holt's face. "You've got Richard Bates. I know that, we all know that. And you want the money and maybe some way to make damn sure another man like him doesn't show up. And then another and another."

Holt stared at the gun in Clint's fist. The other men at the table, all in their fifties like he was, seemed frozen with indecision. Clint wanted to make sure they did not react in error. "Tell your friends that this meal is over before it begins. Tell them to raise their hands and back out the door if you want to live long enough to finish your first cup of coffee."

Enos Holt was headstrong and he was ruthless, but he had no interest in dying. "All right, you men go and do as this—"

Clint cocked the hammer of his gun. "Don't you remember, I don't like to be insulted."

Holt swallowed his bile and growled, "Just get out of here and leave us alone to talk!"

The men pushed back their seats. They were tough, battle-scarred old men, like Holt. They weren't cowards, and they did not like being railroaded or ordered around. Clint could see that in their faces. He knew that they were a hell of a lot more comfortable giving rather than taking orders.

The Gunsmith didn't give a damn. He waited until the men were gone and then he moved a chair around towards the wall where he had a clear field of vision and no one could slip in behind him.

"Now," he said, "you want the money and I want Richard Bates. I propose we work out a fair exchange."

"I have no idea where Bates is. I hope the man is dead and in hell. But if he is, I didn't send him there."

"Stop playing games. Do you really think I'm supposed to believe that the three men I found and killed were upstairs in the Alamo just for fun?"

"Why not? That's one of the places men go in San Antonio."

"Not to my woman's room."

"Are you sure?" Holt asked, suddenly relaxing and enjoying the way the topic of conversation had gone. "Her name is Anita, isn't it? She's just a high-priced whore."

Clint drew back his fist but managed to get himself under

control. This evil old bastard was clever. He looked for a chink in an opponent's armor and then he drove a dagger into the heart.

"Do you know how much money Bates won yesterday?" Clint asked. "Besides what he won from you."

"I have no idea."

"A small fortune. And I know what really grates on you and your friends. Every dime of his winnings came from men like you and the cowboys you hire. Cattlemen and cowboys. Holt, it's easy to see that someone like yourself would consider this his own money. Money rightfully belonging to cattlemen and cowboys. It must really twist your guts to think about how, not only did Bates come in here and beat you in the plaza before everyone, but he took your money and his wire will one day close off your trails!"

Enos Holt's face told Clint he had hit the nail squarely. It wasn't money that had sent Holt into a killing rage down in the plaza, it had been his massive, wounded pride.

"Where is Richard Bates?"

"First things first. Where is our money?" Holt asked.

Clint did not smile. But he knew for sure that Bates was alive. "In a safe place."

"The bank?" Holt asked quickly. Too damned quickly.

Clint smiled. "You and your friends probably own the bank, or at least have a major share of the stock in it. Uh-uh. The bank in this town is not a safe place. It's somewhere else. Somewhere you'll never think to look."

"I want it back," Holt said.

"In exchange for Bates."

"Maybe. If I could believe he'd leave Texas and take his wire with him."

"He'd leave," Clint said. "He'd rather leave than die."

"He's a stubborn sonofabitch and I hate his guts. Just like I hate yours."

Clint shrugged. "I don't give a damn how you feel about me."

Holt pushed the barrel of Clint's gun aside. "Waiter!" he roared. "Where the hell is my breakfast!"

The waiter, on whose shirt Clint had poured the glass of water, vaulted out of the kitchen with a tray, and the food was placed before Holt, who didn't hesitate to dive right into it. He ate like a big, winter-starved wolf. Clint admired the fact that, even with his life in some jeopardy, he had not lost his appetite. Clint's father had always said that a man who could laugh or eat well in spite of danger was a man to be reckoned with at all times.

"Well," Clint asked.

Enos Holt said, "The steak is damned good here, Gunsmith. I eat it three times a day 'cause it makes a man tough, and it comes from my herds."

Clint had not been inquiring about the man's breakfast. Having just had his own steak, he knew it was good. "When do we trade?"

Holt chewed his meat slowly. So slowly that he was either missing some grinding teeth, or else he was afraid of choking on a piece of beef. Clint waited.

"Tell you what," Holt said. "Let's wait a day or two and then, maybe we can do business."

"While you keep torturing Bates? Not a chance."

"Torturing?" Holt made a face. "What kind of a man do you take me for?"

"The kind of man who would shoot a dun bull in the gut and let it die slow and in agony for doing nothing more than fighting for its life."

"You are a real opinionated sonofabitch, Adams. And a very, very dangerous man."

"So I've been told. I just don't think a man like you can stop progress. And I want Bates back alive and healthy."

"I lost a lot of money and so did my friends," Holt said. "I told all my cowhands to bet on the longhorns. I want to pay them back."

"If you can't afford to lose, you shouldn't make the bet," Clint said.

"Oh, I can afford it all right. But it's the way it was done. We don't want wire in Texas."

"It's coming anyway. First Bates, then someone else."

"That may be true," Holt said. "In fact, I figure it probably is true. Now, a smart man would want some time to gain legal ownership to as much range as he could grab before wire came along. But that takes time."

"I see," Clint said. "Yeah, I guess it does take time. Probably months."

"At least," Holt replied.. He sipped at his coffee. "You know, I could file for a couple of thousand acres in your name. You could be well off in a few years if you played along with me and my friends."

Clint could not help smiling. "Tell you what," he said. "Why don't we make our deal, and I'll think it over later."

"That's reasonable," the cattleman said. "I might even forgive you for putting a bullet in my shoulder. That was a hell of a shot with a six-gun. I thought sure you'd used a rifle, but someone who saw you said, no, it was a Colt you fired."

"The same one I'm packing," Clint said.

"I don't want us to be enemies. You won the first go-around, but I've too many men and too damned much power for you to buck. You'll go down hard, but you'll go down."

"When do I get Richard Bates?" Clint asked, weary of sparring with this treacherous old reptile.

"Tomorrow morning. Come out to the ranch."

"Not a chance," Clint said. "We make the exchange right out in front of this hotel. At noon."

"You're out of your mind!"

"That's the way it has to be," Clint said. "If I rode out to your ranch, neither I nor Bates would ever ride out again. Here, or I keep the money and just call San Antonio quits."

"You wouldn't do that."

"Test me," Clint challenged. "Bates isn't even a friend. And that is a lot of money."

"How much?"

"You'll find out tomorrow."

Holt leaned forward. "I figure you'll skim off a few thousand. That's all right. You deserve a cut. Just don't get greedy."

Clint stood up. "Tomorrow at noon."

"At noon," Holt echoed. "You see my friends out in the lobby, tell 'em to come on back and join me for breakfast."

"I'll do that," the Gunsmith said as he walked out of the dining room.

Chapter Ten

The Gunsmith checked his watch. It was a quarter to twelve. He had fifteen minutes left until he met Enos Holt and made a swap for Richard Bates. Clint took his saddlebags and left his room. He went downstairs and then angled out the back door of the hotel and headed down the alley.

When he came to the back door of his little gunshop, Clint swore in anger. The heavy lock had been jimmied and the hinges themselves broken. The door was standing ajar. Clint drew his six-gun and slipped inside the back door. He did not expect the thieves to still be inside, and they were not. Clint walked quickly over to the rifle case and swore again. He had kept a beautiful Remington Rolling-block .50-caliber rifle in there, and it was missing along with several Winchester Model 1873's and a Sharps "Big Fifty" that was worth well over sixty dollars.

There was also a case of pistols in various stages of repair, and they were undisturbed, but two new Peacemakers were gone. All together, Clint estimated his loss at better than two hundred dollars. He was furious. Being a gunsmith, he figured he'd recognize every one of the used guns stolen the first time he saw them. However, the new Peacemakers were a loss.

Clint stomped over to his workbench and opened a few drawers. They had all been disturbed, and when he went to the battered old desk where he kept invoices and a rudimentary filing system, he saw that every drawer had been ransacked.

Clint straightened up, suddenly realizing that, while the thieves had taken firearms, whoever they were had been more interested in finding something else. Obviously, they were looking for Richard Bates' winnings.

"Holt, this makes one more I owe you," he swore, thinking about how Enos Holt must have instructed his men to take weapons in order to avoid suspicion. Clint opened a five-pound tin of black powder. Black powder was still pretty much in demand because a lot of men had not yet traded their old guns in for the newer but more expensive cartridge models. Clint found a little paper sack and poured the entire can into the bag. Then he found a piece of twine. He dipped the twine in a cleaning solvent, letting it soak well, then he made a fuse, which he inserted into the bag of black powder.

Clint could not help chuckling. It was going to be like the Fourth of July and New Year's Eve combined on the main street of San Antonio. Clint used his pocket knife to cut a hole in the bottom of one of the saddlebags, and when he placed the sack of black powder inside, he ran the fuse out through the hole about an inch. Not enough so you'd notice, but enough so that he could light it in a hurry. Clint was not an explosives expert, but he figured it would take the fuse only about ten, maybe even twenty seconds to reach the powder. And after that, there was going to be one hell of a bang.

Satisfied that the bomb would work, Clint covered the powder-sack with old wadded up newspapers, which he also used to fill the other saddlebag. He then slung them over his shoulder, tucking the fuse into his right shirt pocket. From his desk drawer, the Gunsmith located a cigarillo and matches. Glancing at his watch, he figured things were going to become very interesting in a few minutes.

Clint consulted the old pendulum clock over his desk. He had not been here in nearly a week and the clock had stopped. But his pocket watch told him that it was almost noon. Clint rewound and then reset the old clock. When he got the pendulum swinging again, he reached down and lifted his six-gun out of its holster, then eased it back down again. He debated taking a shotgun and decided against that. But he had a nice two-shot derringer, and he slipped that up his sleeve. He hoped it would not come to a war out in the street, because, if it did, he would probably be cut down by riflemen before he could get himself and Bates to cover.

Clint took a deep breath and unlocked his front door. He adjusted the saddlebags once more, then stuffed the thin cigarillo between his lips and lit his smoke. He inhaled only enough to get the cigarillo burning, then he used his tongue to roll it over to one side of his mouth so that the smoke would not waft up into his eyes and in any way alter his vision.

He stepped outside and saw that Enos Holt and his friends were standing in front of the Stockman's House. Clint saw Richard Bates, too, but the Midwesterner was being supported by two burly men. Clint was not pleased. If they had to move fast, it was obvious that Bates was going to be a problem. If the man had been drugged and couldn't even stand on his own two feet, he sure as hell couldn't be expected to run for cover.

Clint stepped off the boardwalk. Wagons and riders were moving up and down the street, and it was obvious that no one really understood what was about to take place. The Gunsmith started walking down toward the Stockman's House. His step was sure, and he pushed back the brim of his Stetson a little to see if he could spot any marksmen up on the rooftops. He saw none, but that didn't mean a thing.

They could be in upstairs hotel rooms hiding just behind curtains.

Enos Holt stepped out and motioned the two men to bring Richard Bates along. They moved about ten feet off the boardwalk and stopped. There was no point in standing directly in the center of the traffic.

"You got what I want in those saddlebags!" Holt called when the Gunsmith drew near.

"I do. But what the hell have you done with him?"

"He's gonna live. There's nothing to worry about."

"Maybe you've poisoned him," Clint growled. "I won't pay until I know he's all right."

Holt reached over and grabbed Richard by the hair. He lifted the man's head so that Clint could see right into his face. It was a face he barely recognized. Bates had been savagely beaten. Both of his eyes were almost completely swollen shut and one cheek was laid open with a nasty gash. His lips were smashed and yet, when Holt wrenched back his head, Bates still tried to smile.

Clint steeled himself to remain under control though his impulse was to kill Enos Holt and then shoot the other two and take his chances. But standing on the porch in front of the Stockman's House were the same group of men that Clint had run out of the dining room. They had rifles, some shotguns, and they had a few other men besides. Clint realized that it didn't matter if there were ambushers on the rooftops or shooting out of windows. If he opened fire, he would never reach safety. There was another sobering thought—even if he killed old man Holt, there were at least five more like him that would have to be reckoned with sooner or later.

"Gunsmith," Bates said thickly. "Get out of here before it's too late."

"It's already too late," Clint said. "Isn't that right, Holt?"

"That's right. You just carry out your part of the bargain and I'll carry out mine. Hand it over."

"Not until you put him on a horse or in the back of a wagon and send him on down the way," Clint said.

Holt just stared at him with hatred. "You're a hard man to do business with."

"Even harder to kill," Clint drawled. Then he stepped in front of a wagon. "Hold it up!"

"Move out of my way!" the wagon driver shouted.

But Clint held his ground. He looked at the old cattleman. "You have those boys throw him up in the back of this wagon, then I'll give you the money. What have you got to lose? If I don't do as I'm supposed to, you can kill me, then run over and shoot him."

The two men looked anxiously at their boss. No doubt they were damned concerned about their own hides. They'd realize that, even if they were both standing with their hands free to draw iron, they'd both be outdrawn by a man as fast as the Gunsmith.

"What the hell is going on here!" the teamster shouted, looking from Clint to Holt, and then at the two men who were keeping Richard on his feet. "Hey, you people got trouble to settle, do it without me! I want nothing to do with any gunplay."

"Do it!" Clint snapped at Holt. "Put him in the back of that wagon, and I'll give you the money."

Holt had no choice. He eyed the saddlebags. "All right," he growled, "throw the bastard in the back."

"Now wait a damn minute!" the teamster shouted. "I don't have to—"

"Shut up or you're a dead man!" Holt bellowed.

The teamster shut up.

Clint waited until the two men started to half-drag, half-carry Richard to the rear of the wagon. Then, as they dumped him into the wagon, the Gunsmith removed the burning cigarillo from his mouth and without attracting any attention, he slipped the cigarillo under the saddlebag and lit the fuse.

Clint hurled the cigarillo to the dirt and ground it out under his heel. He stepped aside for the teamster, who was very eager to whip his team up the street.

"Give me the money!"

"You got it," Clint said, pitching the saddlebags to the cattleman and then backpeddling after the wagon as Holt yanked at the straps.

The ruthless old cattle king chose the saddlebag without the bag of black power, but it really didn't matter. One minute the man was looking inside and his face was changing from expectancy to raw hatred, the next he disappeared in a boom as loud as prairie thunder. A huge cloud of gray smoke obliterated everything, and Clint saw horses and mules going crazy on the street as every living thing tried to distance itself from the explosion.

Clint threw himself into the rear of the freight wagon beside Richard as it began to move faster. He ducked and heard the sound of gunfire, but the men doing the shooting were only adding to the smoke.

When Clint looked a second time, he knew for sure that Enos Holt was gone. Just obliterated.

Clint expelled a deep sigh of relief.

"What happened?" Richard asked in a confused voice.

"The Fourth of July came and went a little fast this year," the Gunsmith said with a tight grin.

He let the freight wagon round the end of the street and then he grabbed Richard and they jumped. Pulling the wire drummer to his feet, he rushed him into the cover of some bushes.

"Can you travel?" he asked the beaten man. "We've got to get out of San Antonio for a little while."

"I can't ride a horse," Richard said. "And I won't leave without my wire or my winnings."

Clint frowned. "Where are they!"

"Wire is buried under the straw at the livery where you keep your horse."

Clint grinned. "That's ingenious. Where's the money?"

"Same livery only in a pair of old saddlebags tied to your saddle."

"You mean . . . just tied to my saddle?"

Richard nodded. "The man who operates the place watches over things close. I figured if I got killed, you'd find the money and send most of it along to my parents in De Kalb, Illinois. There's also a note to Mr. Glidden explaining all about what happened down here and telling him his wire held against those hundred longhorn cattle."

"I underestimated you," Clint said, helping the man back to his feet. "The livery is just a couple hundred yards farther. Can you make it?"

"Do I have any choice?"

"No."

"Then I can make it," Richard said.

Clint helped the man as he struggled along. "What did they drug you with?"

Richard belched and hiccuped. "Whiskey. Rot-gut whiskey, damn 'em!"

Clint shook his head as they struggled toward the livery. "Life is hell sometimes," he grunted.

Chapter Eleven

They managed to reach the livery before they were spotted, but it had taken precious extra minutes and Clint was worried. Several children had seen him helping Richard across the street and into the livery. And while grown-ups were inclined to mind their own business in the face of danger, there was no way that the children would remain quiet if asked about two men running on foot, one holding up the other.

"We don't have much time," Clint said, racing inside and dropping Richard while he went for his saddle.

"Hey," the liveryman yelled, "is that you, Mr. Adams?"

"Sure is!" Clint had to search his memory to recall that the man's name was Bert. Bert had to be seventy years old if he was a day. He had big, work-roughened hands and a gentle way with horses and mules. Stiff bones and age had probably retired him from cowboying as much as twenty or thirty years ago.

"Well, what are you all out of breath for?"

"We're being chased, Bert. I just blew up Enos Holt. I suspect every damn one of his friends are after us."

Bert's jaw dropped. "Ya blew him up? Finished off the old fart?"

Clint nodded as he shoved his way into a little room where Bert kept his boarders' tack under lock and key. The light was bad, but Clint knew which saddle rack his gear was on and when he found the saddlebags, he opened them by feel and plunged his hands into a wad of money big enough to start a bonfire.

"Is it still there?" Richard called.

"It sure is," the Gunsmith replied, rebuckling the straps and yanking his saddle off the rack. He also grabbed his blanket and bridle.

"You taking Duke out?" Bert asked.

Clint almost ran to the stall. "Yeah. But what I need is that buckboard out on your back lot and a couple of fast horses to pull it. I'm in a hurry, Bert. If they track us down to here, it'll go bad for everyone."

"I hated that Enos Holt," Bert said. "I'm glad he cashed it in before me. He always said he'd live the longer. But I don't guess he ever—"

"Come on, Bert!" Clint yelled. "We're running out of time! Get a team of horses and get the buckboard hitched up!"

Bert stepped a little quicker, but not much. And while Clint saddled Duke and then dove into the straw pile and retrieved what little remained of the spool of barbed wire, the old fella collected a set of harness and trudged out to catch a couple of horses and get them hitched up to the buckboard.

"We'll have to buy the buckboard, the horses, and the harness," Clint said. "I don't expect to be coming back for a while—if we get out of this town alive."

"Then buy them," Richard said. "Take a fistful of dollars out of those saddlebags and pay the man whatever he wants. Pay your horse's feed and boarding bill, too."

Clint smiled grimly. "You're feeling pretty generous for a man who has just had the hell beaten out of him."

"When you see how much money I won, you'll understand." Richard seemed to be sobering up a little. He went over to what was left of his spool of barbed wire and studied it carefully. "That was pretty damn clever with those exploding saddlebags. Holt was a rabid animal that needed destroying. But there are some others in this town almost as bad."

"We can come back for them on our terms," Clint said. "Right now, you're in no condition to fight, and all the odds are with them."

Richard chuckled. "After hearing about you so much and seeing what you did. I'm almost beginning to think you're invincible. That long odds don't matter, and you'll always find a way to win."

Clint shook his head and tightened his cinch. He would tie Duke to the back of the buckboard. It wasn't a good arrangement, but he had no intention of leaving the horse behind. "The minute I ever get so dumb as to figure I can't be stopped is when I get planted."

"Have we got any chance at all of getting out of San Antonio alive?"

"Sure we do! If our luck holds, we'll make it just fine. But we haven't much time, and I'm afraid old Bert is not helping matters much."

Clint finished saddling his horse. He handed the reins to Richard. "Hold him while I go and help Bert."

Richard took the reins with some reluctance. It was clear that he had not been around horses very much. "Does it bite?"

" 'It' has a name and that name is Duke," Clint said on his way outside. "He's a gentleman who would no more bite you than you would him."

Outside, Clint found Bert standing with one boot on the lower rail of the corral. The man eyed him and said, "I'm afraid all I got is some wind-broken old nags I'm ashamed to sell you."

"I'll take the sorrel and the bay," Clint said, moving through the rails to catch the horses. "And you're right, they are nearly worthless, but we're desperate."

"I guess you are," Bert said, his mind working swiftly as he handed Clint the harness once he had both horses haltered and under control. "You gonna buy 'em or rent 'em?"

"I may not be back for a while," Clint said. "So I'll buy."

Bert's rheumy old eyes brightened a little. "You are in a fix, but I won't try and take advantage of you none."

"Take advantage if you want," Clint told the man as they began to harness up the sorry-looking team, "it isn't my money."

"It's the dude's, is it? The same money he won in the plaza?"

"Yep."

Bert spat tobacco juice into the dust. "That fancy sonofabitch must have won ten thousand dollars or more."

"At least," Clint agreed.

Bert thought on that for several minutes. "I guess I'm going to have to have a hundred dollars for these two horses."

It was outrageous, but Clint didn't care, and he suspected Richard wouldn't either since their lives hung in the balance.

"Then, I'll need another hundred for the buckboard. It's in good shape, you know."

When Clint didn't howl, Bert pushed his luck. "And that harness, well, it's the finest you can buy. Made by a Mexican leather worker named Miguel Flores. A set of harness like that is hard to find."

"How much?"

This time, Bert couldn't even look the Gunsmith in the eye. "Another hundred would be jest fine, thank you."

"So we're up to three hundred?"

"Yes, sir!"

"It's a deal."

Bert looked stunned. "You're gonna just pay it without a fuss or nothing?"

"If you throw in my board bill for Duke. Yep, we'll pay."

Bert grinned broadly. "Well, I'll be damned. You got a deal!"

Clint led the two horses out of the corral and backed them up to the buckboard. "You hitch the team up while I get Richard, the wire, and my horse."

"And three hundred dollars!"

"And that, too," Clint called back.

He stepped into the dim interior of the barn and suddenly, he heard Richard grunt a warning. Grunt because he was on the ground with a gag stuffed in his mouth and fresh blood running down the side of his face.

Clint tried to jump out of the way, but he was a fraction of a second too late. A man waiting just inside the door swung a piece of wood at his head, and Clint took it across the back of his skull. He dropped, half stunned as the cattlemen rushed to pin him to the dirt floor of the barn and tear his gun out of its holster.

"You've lost," a man said, sounding as if he were speaking from a great distance. "We found the money and there's plenty enough barbed wire to hang you both from the rafters of this here barn."

Clint tried to move but couldn't. He was dazed, and there wasn't much hope that he could get out of this mess alive.

It seemed his good luck had just turned bad.

Chapter Twelve

Clint was jerked unceremoniously to his feet. Two men had to support him while he was searched. His six-gun and derringer were found.

One of the men laughed in Clint's face. "Where you're going, you won't need these. I'd say these two weapons ought to be worth a hell of a lot of money, given the fact that you're famous. Maybe we'll cut some notches in the handles and that'd even make 'em worth a whole lot more. How many men you shot and killed, Gunsmith?"

Clint tried to raise his head and focus. It felt as if the inside of his skull had been scrambled. Even his eyes ached, and he seemed to see the men around him as if through water. "Go to hell," he said thickly.

The cowboy slapped his face. Clint felt his legs go out from under him and tasted blood in his mouth.

"He sure don't seem to be such a dangerous man right now," someone said, causing the others to laugh.

Clint said nothing. He needed a few seconds to clear his brain of the cobwebs. The interior of the barn was dim, and Duke was nervous as the men crowded in on Clint. He looked at his enemies and counted no less than a dozen. There were four or five older men, obviously ranchers, and the rest were hard-looking cowboys.

One of the prominent-appearing cattlemen stepped forward. He was in his fifties, lean and an easy six-footer with a hooked nose and a nasty scar through one of his eyebrows. There was a wildness in his eyes when he spoke to the Gunsmith. "My name is Duclaw. Rance Duclaw. You outsmarted Enos, and you killed three pretty fair gunmen so it gives me a hell of a lot of satisfaction to see you hang."

Clint saw Richard Bates lying facedown in the straw, knocked out cold. "You might be able to justify killing me, Duclaw, but what about Richard Bates? He never killed anyone. All he's guilty of is winning your money."

"He's guilty of a hell of a lot more than that," Duclaw spat. "He's guilty of trying to kill off the northern trails. He's guilty of not giving a goddam about the cowboy and the cattle industry down here in Texas. He's for the farmer and the sodbuster. The small-minded and the weak-minded."

"No he isn't," Clint argued, bidding for precious time to clear his own head as well as think of some way to get out of this mess. "Bates is for the right for a man to own and work his own section of land in peace. To plant corn or wheat and raise his kids strong and honestly. To see a fair harvest in return for the sweat of his brow."

"Shut the sonofabitch up, Rance!" one of the other cattlemen shouted. "Or by God, I'll shoot him in the mouth."

"Let's get the hanging over with," said another.

Clint glanced back down at Richard. He was still unconscious. The Gunsmith returned his attention to Duclaw, who seemed to be in command. "What kind of a man would hang another while he was unconscious?" Clint said, trying to force some bluster into his voice. "What are you going to do, hoist Bates up in the air when he doesn't even know he's dying? Do that and you'll be haunted all the rest of your life."

Duclaw frowned. "Maybe that's true enough. It'll give us no satisfaction hanging him if he's out cold. Might as well strangle him where he lies."

Duclaw shouted, "Someone get a bucket of water and pour it over his head."

A cowboy went to get the bucket. Clint's mind raced. He tried to think of every way imaginable to get out of this mess but absolutely nothing came to his mind.

"We found the money in your saddlebags," Rance Duclaw said with a smug look on his rugged face. "Jeb, you boys counted it all out yet?"

"Not yet," a voice called, "but we got up to eighteen thousand dollars so far, and that's not but a little more than half of it!"

Even Duclaw was impressed. "Enos kept telling me that the bets totaled over thirty thousand dollars. That Illinois sonofabitch thought he could come down here to Texas and fleece us with his wire, then go the hell back where he came from and tell everyone what fools there was down this way. Ain't going to happen, Gunsmith. We don't like being made to look bad."

"That's all smoke and you know it," Clint said. "You men are nothing but thieves and murderers. You lost your bet and you want your money back. It's that simple."

"Make a couple of nooses out of that wire," Duclaw growled. "We're gonna throw the ends over the rafters and run the Gunsmith and his friend up like a couple of dirty Union flags."

The other men looked nervous, but they were in this all the way, and Clint knew it was going to be impossible to divert their loyalties.

The cowboy who had gone to fetch the bucket of water finally reappeared. "Here it is, Mr. Duclaw."

Rance took the water and poured it over Richard Bates' face. The Midwesterner spluttered and came awake, but anyone could see that he was still dazed.

Duclaw glanced aside. "You boys got the nooses ready yet?"

"Not yet. This damned wire is tough to work with. Keeps sticking us with them barbs."

"Hurry up!" Duclaw ordered. "We want to get this done with."

"The word will get out," Clint gritted. "People will hear about this murderous act. I know that the law in San Antonio is in your back pocket, but when the Texas Rangers come to investigate. . . ."

"They'll find nothing but a huge pile of cold ashes. And your bones," Duclaw said. "Because as soon as we have the pleasure of watching you and your friend kick yourselves into eternity, we'll burn this whole goddam place down. Won't be any evidence of a hanging or anything else."

"Mr. Duclaw, we count thirty-one thousand fifty-five dollars!"

The figure was staggering. "Sonofabitch," Duclaw whispered. "I didn't think there was that much money in this whole goddam town! At least, not in the spring before the cattle are driven north to sell."

"What are we going to do with it?"

Duclaw did not want to talk about that right now. "We'll work out something fair for all of us," he snapped. "Right now, we got ourselves a hanging to do, and that's all that I want to think about. Are the nooses finally ready?"

"Yeah, but they ain't gonna work right. What we're gonna do is just wind up strangling the poor bastards."

Clint felt a chill sweep through him. He had seen plenty of hangings. They were always gruesome, but never so much as when the hangman's knot failed to break the condemned man's neck and kill him instantly. To see a live man choke and strangle, fight and kick while the life and his bodily fluids drained out of him was enough to turn anyone's stomach. Maybe some of the cowboys present had seen that happen as well, because when the Gunsmith's eyes swept across their faces, they looked ashamed and like they wanted no part of this.

One cowboy even said as much. "I'd just as soon see 'em both shot as choke to death."

But Rance Duclaw had obviously figured out what he wanted and nobody was going to change his plan. "We hang 'em. And when the barn fire cools, they'll find the bodies—or what's left of them—with wire around their necks. Sure, it'll tell everybody that they was hung. But they'll be no evidence, and I want every man present to lay a hand on the wire that hoists them up to the rafters. Nobody is going to get out of being a part of this. And the wire around their neckbones will serve a warning that will never be forgotten. We'll have no more men from Illinois or anywhere else coming down here with that damned stuff."

Clint looked at Richard Bates. To the young man's credit, he was standing tall and straight. There was fear—almost uncontrolled fear—in his eyes, but Clint knew that Richard Bates was not going to beg or scream or disgrace himself before death.

The Gunsmith craned his head back and looked up at the rafters as two lengths of barbed wire were thrown neatly over their dusty girths. The rafter from which they'd hang was about fifteen feet off the ground, and it was very stout.

"Get a horse for Bates," Duclaw said, his voice firm but quiet now that he had given his orders and knew that they would be followed. "Gunsmith, you can make your last ride on your own horse sitting in your own saddle."

Wild hope flared in Clint. The moment he got in the saddle, he'd kick Duke in the ribs and try to drive the gelding through the bunch of them and out the rear door. Sure, he'd probably be shot before he could get clear, but a bullet was infinitely more appealing than the crazed horror of being hung by barbed wire.

"Put the noose around him before he ever gets near that horse," Duclaw ordered, "and make sure that half of you men grab the wire between the barbs. If the bastard wants to make his horse run, then stand aside and let him. Once he's swinging, let's hoist him up halfway."

The cowboys and other cattlemen licked their lips nervously. A second horse was haltered for Richard and led out of its stall. "You can ride bareback. I'll guarantee you that you won't ride far enough to get sore," a cowboy said.

It was said as a joke, but no one laughed.

The wire noose was placed over Richard's neck. Clint was close enough to see how the barbs dug into the man's flesh and raised drops of blood. A noose was put over his own neck and Clint felt the bite of it. He wanted to kick and struggle, but he knew that he was helpless at least until he was on his horse. Maybe then, maybe by some miracle . . . but what miracle? Duclaw was too smart. Even if he did try and escape, he would hang.

Duclaw looked at Clint. "You fell in with the wrong side of this, Gunsmith. I wish you hadn't, for we had no quarrel with you until you started killing our men."

"They came for me, what was I supposed to do? Let them put a bullet in me or rape Anita?"

Duclaw shook his head. "I don't know about all of that. I just know for sure that all the talking is done. Get on your horse and die like a man. We know you're no coward. Prove it."

Clint swallowed hard and climbed into his saddle. He felt the wire tighten and the barbs cut into his throat. He had always wondered how he would die, but never in his worst nightmares had it been as terrible as this.

"Remember," Duclaw said. "We hoist 'em up and then

we set the fire. I don't want none of you boys to fire the straw until this is done."

The unmistakable sounds of the twin hammers of a double-barreled shotgun being cocked were followed by the words, "You murderin' sonofabitches think you can just walk in here and burn *my* place to the ground! Hell no, you can't!"

"Bert," Duclaw shouted, "have you gone crazy? Put that shotgun down!"

"I won't do it," the old liveryman said. "This is wrong. All wrong. You can't burn me out and kill those two."

"Pay the old bastard," a man whispered. "Give him a thousand dollars to turn around and get the hell out of here!"

Duclaw nodded. "Listen Bert, we were gonna pay for the barn."

"Like hell you was! You never asked me about any of this. You boys just come in here and kill them two men and then burn me out."

"A thousand dollars," Duclaw said. "That's more than this rickety old barn was ever worth."

"Not enough."

"All right, two thousand."

"It's blood money," Bert hissed.

Duclaw swore. "Bert, if you foul this up, you know you're finished in San Antonio. You'll be shot instead of just being run out of town."

"I know," the old man said. He looked up at Clint. "Gunsmith, how much is my business worth?"

Clint managed to croak, "Ten thousand dollars, Bert. This fine old barn and all the years you put into it ought to be worth ten thousand dollars."

"Bates, it's your winnings, you agree?"

Richard Bates nodded emphatically. "I sure do."

Rance Duclaw blustered, "Now just a goddam—"

"Out!" Bert shouted. "All of you men out and the first

one that reaches for those saddlebags dies for them."

No one, not Rance Duclaw or any of the other cattlemen were quite ready to die for the money.

"You're a dead man, Bert," Rance spat. "We'll kill you and then this pair. It's just a matter of where and when. Just where and when, Bert. You'll never live to spend that ten thousand. You better think this over."

"Already have. Now git! All of you!"

Duclaw was beaten and knew it, but it wasn't his way to tuck his tail between his legs and slink out. He said, "If either of you are ever seen in Texas again, you're both dead men. There isn't a town in this state where one of us don't have friends. Cattlemen stick together. Try to sell a single yard of your damned wire again, you're finished."

"I sure don't like threats," the Gunsmith said. "I don't like them at all. A man who makes threats had better be able to back them up."

"I can back up anything I say and so can the other men standing behind me. And as far as not liking threats, it makes no difference to me what you like, or don't like," Duclaw said. "If you and your pretty friend can get out of Texas before we catch you, then I guess you'll live a little longer. But we'll be hunting you. I wouldn't give odds any one of the three of you could get out of this town, much less the state, before we find you."

Clint's voice hardened. "You already proved how smart of a gambler you were when you bet against barbed wire. I don't run, Duclaw, and, if Richard wants to sell wire in Texas, it's a free country, and I guess I'll help him sell the damned stuff just to make that point."

"You're brave, but stupid," Duclaw said. "Every town you come into, there'll be a man waiting. A gunman, a cattleman, some cowboys. We'll see that you're stopped. If not at our city limits, then at someone else's. You want to sell wire with this drummer as your partner, then go somewhere far away. Maybe out in California or back to the Midwest. Just stay the hell out of cattle country!"

Duclaw turned to Bert. "You rotten, worthless old bastard," he hissed. "Enos never liked you and now I know why. You're traitor to Texas!"

Bert spat a stream of tobacco juice in the cattleman's face. "Turn around and get off my property while you're still breathing."

Duclaw turned and walked out and the others followed him. Clint heaved a deep sigh of relief. "Old man," he said, "you have saved our lives."

Bert nodded. "The question I'm asking you is, are the two of you worth ten thousand dollars and all the grief this is going to bring my way?"

Clint removed the wire noose from around his cut neck. "We are," he said, "and you'll live long enough to spend your money. That's a promise."

"I'll second that promise," Bates said as he slipped the wire from around his neck and then dismounted. He looked up at the two trailers of wire that were looped over the rafter. "This is one use for his invention that Mr. Glidden need never know about."

Clint nodded. He could not agree more.

Chapter Thirteen

They stood quietly, waiting for darkness to fall so that they might at least have some chance of escaping the barn and then getting out of San Antonio. But Clint was caught in a quandary. It was his nature to hunt, rather than to be hunted. Every fiber of his being railed against being chased from San Antonio. Had there simply been his own life to consider, he would have stayed and fought. Fought Rance Duclaw and anyone else who tried to tell him what he could or could not do in Texas.

But there were two other lives at stake, those of Richard Bates and the old liveryman, Bert. Neither man was capable of saving himself. So Clint figured that he owed those two a chance of escape. After that, well, he'd come back here some day and settle the odds. He wasn't forgetting how he'd almost been brained and then strangled. And though his head had been foggy and his ears had rung, he would remember most of the faces of those who had been here and had seemed so damned eager to see him swing from the rafters.

Richard had taken an awful beating. He would not be recognized as the brash, overconfident man who had arrived in San Antonio only a short time ago. A young, handsome, ambitious man who had naively thought he could sell barbed

99

wire in the heart of cattle country.

Now, Bates seemed rather subdued. He sat on the straw beside the saddlebags filled with money, and he had a faraway look in his eyes. Bert, however, seemed almost cheerful.

"If I'm gonna get shot trying to leave this town, at least they'll be killin' a rich man," he said. "Ten thousand dollars! Why that's more than I made in my whole life. More than I made and my Pa made all put together! I wish my Pa was alive to see me and this money."

Clint glanced over at the old man. "Why?"

"I just do," Bert said with a wide, nearly toothless grin. "You see, he always said that if I became a cowboy, I'd wind up either stomped to death, crippled up before my time, or dead broke and without nothing or nobody to show for my life."

"He was wrong," Clint said. "This is a fine old barn, and you run a good stable. And now you're worth ten thousand dollars."

Richard had already paid Bert his money. Gladly paid it. Now, Bert couldn't keep from playing with it, counting it over and over, feeling the hundred-dollar bills and just enjoying the touch of the actual currency. Clint had seen a few poor old men come into big money, and Bert's fascination with that much currency was not unusual.

"Oh," the old man said, "I did better than Pa said I'd do. A damn sight better. But gettin' rich like this, at my age, well, it's something I'd given up even thinking about."

Bert looked over at Richard, "You hold no hard feelings against me, do you, young feller?"

Richard shook his head and smiled. "Of course not. Without you, we'd be dead."

"Yes, you would be," Bert said agreeably. "Besides, you still got over twenty thousand there. That's a lot of money.

Enough to last two lifetimes, if you didn't spend it all on the whores and the whiskey."

Richard forced a smile that was painful to see. He reached into the saddlebags and pulled out the money. He absently stacked it into two even piles and shoved one at Clint. "Did you mean what you said about helping me sell wire down here in Texas?"

"I don't give a damn about wire," Clint admitted. "In fact, the idea of closing off land goes against my grain. But I do believe that people have a right to protect what they own and that your wire will make that possible. So, yes. I'll help you sell wire in Texas, but I'll do it by keeping you alive."

"How?"

"What do you mean?"

Richard frowned. "Well, you heard what Duclaw said."

"You mean about how we'll be hunted and hounded no matter where we go in Texas?"

"Yeah," Richard said. "So I guess I better try another state. I'm not a coward, but I'm not anxious to die, either."

"Is it in your nature to run?" Clint asked.

"Hell, no, it isn't!" Richard lowered his voice. "But we could try Colorado, then New Mexico. Why, there's the whole wide West to sell wire to, Clint. We'll sell a million miles of it and then return to Texas. By then, we'd be so well known they couldn't touch us."

"Only you wouldn't return," Clint said. "By the time you'd sold that much wire, you'd be too damn rich to want to take a chance anymore. And in the meantime, some other poor devil would come down here and get tarred and feathered—or worse. You'd think about that, and it would eat at you until you weren't the same man you are now. And you'd know that running away was a mistake. It most always is."

"Dammit," Bates said, "you're right. But I'm not like you. I'm no gunfighter. I'm just a barbed wire salesman."

"You're a damn sight more than that," Clint said. "You have ice in your veins. It took a lot of courage to come into this town and stage that contest, knowing you would be lynched if you lost."

"I almost was anyway."

"Doesn't change a thing," Clint said. "The only thing I'm saying is this: If you're going to sell wire, you're going to have to learn how to defend yourself with a gun. Maybe I can teach you."

"You mean to kill?"

Clint shrugged. "Sometimes, it's either you or the man who challenges you. I'll stick with you for a while. Try to get through all this. But I'm going to want to come back here and pay a few debts to Mr. Duclaw and a couple of his men. If you come with me, you'll have to know how to use a gun."

Richard nodded. "All this talk assumes that we'll survive an escape attempt tonight. Right now, that seems to be a pretty large assumption."

"I suppose it is at that," Clint said. He turned to Bert. "Any ideas, old man? That ten thousand would sure be fun to spend if you can figure a way to get us past the men who will ring this barn."

"There ain't no way except to line the inside of the buck-board with some of that old scrap iron I got stacked up right over there in the corner. Hitch up a couple of horses, get into the buckboard and let 'er rip! We'd make it through their ring, but I don't know what we'd do after that."

Clint grinned broadly. "That's a pretty fair idea! We can worry about what to do after we escape later. Can you both ride a horse?"

"Maybe at a walk," Richard said, not sounding at all confident.

"Hell, yes," Bert said grumpily. "But I said we'd have to lie down in the buckboard."

"That's right," Clint replied. "But once we're through the ring, we'll have to move fast. Richard, you're going to have to try. I don't think they'll chase us too far in the night."

"I'm game," he said.

"Bert?"

"Let's get busy," the old man said. "I jest hope that they didn't move the buckboard when they were fixing to hang you boys. I had it just outside the door, all hitched up and everything."

Clint went to the back door and peered out. The team and the buckboard were just ten feet away. But a man could get killed in that ten feet. In fact, Clint had no doubt that was exactly what would happen.

"We got a problem," he said.

"No problem at all," Bert replied. "Take some of that damned sugar you're always feeding your horse and hold it out flat on your palm so them two horses can see it. They'll come."

Clint did as he was told. Both the sorrel and the bay eyed the sugar warily, then looked away. "They don't even know what sugar is!"

Bert scrubbed his beard with his work-thickened fingers. "They damn sure know what carrots are," he grumbled.

In a few moments he was back with two long carrots. "You watch how this pair of sweethearts take notice now."

Bert was right. The moment the sorrel and the bay saw the carrots, they lurched forward in their harness and before any of the men outside could yell or even shoot, the animals were inside, teeth chomping on the carrots as Clint hauled them and the buckboard all the way into the barn.

"Nice work," Clint said, heading for the pile of scrap metal. "Now let's see what we can do to keep ourselves from being riddled with bullets."

The wagon was ready. Rance Duclaw and the cattlemen outside must have wondered mightily what the hell was going on inside the barn with all the banging around and the hammering. But because of the Gunsmith's reputation, no one dared to come close to the livery barn, and now, the moment of escape was at hand.

Clint tied a thirty-foot long lariat around his gelding's neck, then fastened the rope to the back of the buckboard. Bullets would be fired at the buckboard, and he did not want Duke to be anywhere close when the shooting started and they made their bid for freedom.

"I'll handle the team," Bert said to the Gunsmith. "Best thing you can do is to stay in the back and use those guns I gave you and the dude."

Clint agreed. "Just stay down and keep the team moving, old-timer. If we can get to the cover of the river, we can ditch the wagon and ride our horses to safety."

"Easy for you to say," Bert grumbled. "You're the only one of the three of us with a horse worth spit."

"Life is hard and unfair sometimes," Clint said, not being very sympathetic.

Bert nodded his head. "Let's find out how hard it gets right now."

Clint looked at Richard. "You ready?"

"As ready as I can get," he said. "I hope you don't figure I'm going to hit anyone that I aim for."

"Nope. Just keep your head down, stick your gun over the sides and pull the trigger until it's empty, then reload and do it again. We just want them to think twice about coming after us."

Richard climbed stiffly into the wagon. He had been beaten so badly that he probably had a few broken ribs, but he wouldn't complain.

Clint headed for the front door of the livery barn. They would make their dash for freedom heading onto the main street, and he would have to leap into the buckboard as it left the barn. It would be tricky, but there was no alternative.

He studied the buckboard once, judging its strength and figuring it would have to do. The wagon had originally been built with very low sides of thin wood, which were only just high enough to keep boxes from bouncing out. Clint and Bert had used the scrap iron to build the sides up to a height of nearly two feet. Plenty high enough to give them cover.

"I hope this metal is thick enough to deflect their fire," Richard said.

"Trust me. It's thick enough to stop anything smaller than a .50-caliber slug. And they won't be shooting any cannons."

Bert climbed into the seat and got the horses lined up to charge the big front doors the moment that Clint yanked them wide open. The Gunsmith peeked outside. Darkness was just starting to fall, and the light was bad for shooting.

"Anytime you're ready!" Bert shouted, edging off his seat and ducking into the bed.

The bay and the sorrel could sense that something dramatic was about to occur. And though well past their prime, both animals had their heads up and they looked alert, ready to run.

Clint grabbed the right door. "Here we go!"

Bert had warned him that the doors had to be lifted but he had not said how hard. Clint threw his shoulder into the weight of the huge door and muscled it open. He raced back, grabbed the left-hand door and slammed it forward as the first bullets came streaking his way.

"Yaaah!" Bert shouted, reaching over the driver's seat to send a long bullwhip cracking over the two already frightened horses. The bay and sorrel bolted out of their tracks as if they were born to run. They shot through the door so fast it was all that Clint could do to get a hand on the tailgate of the buckboard and swing himself up into its bed.

Bullets were whap-whapping the metal sides of the buckboard and sounding exactly like hail beating against a tin roof. "Stay down!" Clint shouted.

"What else?" Richard yelled as the buckboard slewed around a corner and down the street, first on two wheels of one side, then two wheels on the other.

Clint and Richard had open firing out the back, taking care to avoid shooting Duke, who galloped easily along behind the wagon as if he was on some kind of a Sunday lark. Clint triggered off three quick shots. Not that he actually had any illusions that he could hit anyone. That was impossible, given the way the buckboard was careening from side to side.

"Yee haw!" Bert shouted, as the wagon passed through the hail of lead and slewed wildly into the street. "We did it! We—"

A rifle bullet struck the old man between the shoulder blades, and Bert stiffened, his arms lifting to the sky. Clint caught him before he fell, knowing Bert was already dead. There was nothing he could do for Bert, so he lunged for the lines, but it was too late. They were dragging somewhere under the wagon and the team was racing out of control.

"Hang on for your life!" Clint shouted. An instant later, he changed his mind as a big freight wagon moved into their path. "Jump!" Clint cut Duke loose in a split second.

Richard and he both jumped at the same instant as the sorrel and the bay swerved sharply to avoid hitting the freight wagon. The buckboard whipped sideways for a moment, then flipped over and over and crashed into the freight wagon.

Clint hit the ground on his feet and rolled. Richard was hurled into a water trough and didn't move. The street was suddenly in chaos. The freighter was yelling, while Rance Duclaw and his men were running on foot down the street, firing their guns, and people were scattering to take cover.

Clint staggered over and grabbed Richard under the arms. He threw him across a good-looking palomino tied to a hitching rail, then used the saddle tie strings to lash Richard in place. He untied the palomino, swung onto Duke, and they were off and racing down the street with bullets flying in every direction.

They were going to make it. But Bert hadn't. That was one more Clint figured he owed Duclaw and his henchmen. They'd get Bert's ten thousand dollars, too.

Damn!

Clint looked back over his shoulder and he let Duke run. Richard was taking a hell of a bad pounding and, if he already had broken ribs, Clint prayed that a rib did not puncture his lungs. But there was no help for this. They had to put some distance between themselves and San Antonio.

Clint turned Duke toward the river. He would follow it to wash out their tracks. And someplace before daylight, he would have to find medical help and a sanctuary for Richard—if he hadn't already died of a broken neck when he was thrown into that water trough.

Clint wished he could take the time to stop and check to see if Richard was still alive. But that wasn't possible. So he gave Duke his head and let the animal gallop swiftly into the falling darkness. At least he had picked a good horse for Richard this time. The animal was laboring mightily to keep up with the black gelding, and it was doing an honest and creditable job.

Maybe, the Gunsmith thought, my luck is already starting to turn around again. But they'll pay for Bert.

They can damn sure bet on it.

Chapter Fourteen

Clint eased Duke into a walk and entered the river, then followed it upstream for almost two hours. Satisfied that he would have thrown anyone off his trail, the Gunsmith exited the river and rode north up toward the Llano Estacado. He was looking for high, cool country where there was good water, food, and game to hunt. Along the way, he hoped to find a doctor in one of the many small settlements that had been founded and were flourishing since Civil War veterans had returned to Texas to stand up against the marauding Comanche and Kiowa.

The Gunsmith thought about all that had happened back in San Antonio, and what might happen when he one day returned to avenge the death of Bert and repay Duclaw and his friends for their inhospitality. Clint marveled at how things could change so fast in a man's life. Hell, before Richard Bates and his damned barbed wire, things had been going real fine. Clint had Anita, and he had his own gunsmith shop when he tired of playing cards.

I can't blame Richard, he reminded himself. After all, the young salesman from Illinois had thought he was going to change the face of the West with his damned barbed wire. What had happened hadn't been his fault. But it once again reminded the Gunsmith that, like so many other things in life, one man's actions caused either ill or good for another man. In Bert's case, it had caused death. In Anita's case, a beating, a near rape, and then a hurried stagecoach ride to Austin. In Clint's own case, barbed wire had damned near gotten him hung. He could still feel the soreness around his neck where the barbs had bitten into his flesh.

Clint considered going to Austin, but as he surveyed the chill stars overhead, he knew that that would be a poor idea. He would put Anita's life in further jeopardy. So the best he could do was to see that Richard received medical attention and then try to convince the man that selling barbed wire—no matter how revolutionary the product might be— was a terminal occupation in Texas.

It was long after midnight when the Gunsmith heard Richard groan. Clint rode a few more miles until he reached the Guadalupe River. He dismounted and let Duke and the palomino drink their fills.

"Gunsmith," Richard said in a weak voice. "I'm dying in this position. Get me down!"

Clint untied the man and helped him to the ground. He removed his hat and used it to carry water to the man's side. "Here, drink," Clint ordered.

Richard was in pain and he was ill, but he was alert. "I'll be damned if I'll drink out of your dirty old hat."

"Suit yourself. Crawl over to the river and drink your fill."

To Clint's surprise, Richard was able to climb to his feet and staggered over to the water where he knelt. The man cupped his hands and used them like a dipper to drink his fill.

"You don't have broken ribs after all," Clint said.

Richard finished drinking his fill. "What made you think I did?"

"The beating you took in the barn coupled with being tied over the saddle when we left San Antonio on the run."

"I want to return to San Antonio as soon as the time is right," Richard said. "I want to pay them back for killing Bert."

"We'll go back," Clint said. "But not until you're ready."

"You mean until I learn to handle a gun?"

Clint nodded his head. "Until then, I figure that the best thing for you to do is to take it easy. Rest and—"

"No," Richard said quickly. "I want to order some more barbed wire and keep selling it."

Clint was not pleased, yet he was not surprised, either. "If you do that, we'll have nothing but trouble. Remember what Duclaw said about having friends all over Texas? We'll never know where or when a bullet is coming with our name on it."

"Are we on the way to Austin?"

"No." Clint chose his words carefully. "Listen to me. I'll stick with you and I'll even help you sell wire. But first, you have to mend a little. If you could see your face, you'd understand. We'll rest up in the hill country. Find us a place to hole up and take it easy for a few weeks while you learn to handle a gun."

"You seem to have it all figured out," Richard said, his voice sounding a little stretched.

"No, I don't. But I do know this. When it came to the gunplay back in San Antonio, you were as helpless as a lamb. It's time you learned to shoot fast and straight. Either that, or you might as well go back to Illinois. I see no point in helping a man who refuses to help himself stay alive."

Richard Bates frowned. He glanced up at the moonlight and gingerly explored his face with his fingertips. "I'm not a violent man," he said. "I hate killing, and I've never felt comfortable with guns. But this is Texas. I'll try."

"Good." Clint checked his cinch and advised Richard to do the same. "We've got some riding to do yet. Where we're going it's pretty but hard country. It belongs to the Comanche, and they still raid and take plenty of scalps each year."

"Barbed wire will change all that," Richard said confidently. "Barbed wire will pacify the American Indian quicker than bullets. It will turn them into peaceful farmers no longer dependent on a meager hunting subsistence."

Clint didn't agree and he said so. "They did just fine as hunters until the whites came in and killed off most of their buffalo. By the time that barbed wire is widely accepted and fences off the trails, the buffalo will long since have been extinct."

"Give me just ten years," Richard said.

"Okay," Clint said, "but what you don't understand yet, is that buffaloes haven't even got that much time left. They're damn near all gone."

They mounted up again and rode on, each man lost in his own private thoughts. Clint thought about Anita and wished he was riding toward Austin. Richard Bates thought about Illinois and a girl named Milly. He was secretly home-sick. He also felt as if he had failed in San Antonio. Oh sure, he'd built his fence in the plaza and barbed wire had emerged victorious over a hundred head of the wildest long-horn cattle in Texas. The newspapers across Texas had gotten the story out and yet, there would still be dis-believers. Men who thought that the barbed wire was crazy and impractical.

No, Richard thought, I won in the plaza, but the real battle to gain converts is just beginning.

"Clint?"

The Gunsmith looked over at the Midwesterner. "Yeah?"

"I want you to know something. You saved my life, and you're going to help me make history."

Clint smiled and shook his head. "If we aren't careful, we'll *be* history the next time we run into a group of powerful cattlemen."

"It'll be different from now on," Richard promised. "I

can see that you're right about guns. There's nothing wrong with guns, only the way some men use them. Use them to kill, intimidate, and hold power over other men."

"That's true."

"I've heard you are the fastest man alive with a six-gun. Is that also true?"

"Probably not," Clint admitted. "Somewhere, there's a younger man than either of us. And he's practicing his fast draw six, eight hours a day. If he's got some money, he's spending it all on cartridges. He wants a reputation. Perhaps even my reputation. All he has to do is to challenge me and stop me from walking away. Then he just has to beat me. There's always someone who can beat you on a given day."

"But you keep beating them," Richard argued. "I've heard that you've had over a dozen gunfighters come at you like that and you've never been beat. A dozen!"

"It only takes one," Clint said quietly. "And if I had it all to do over again, I'd have started out as a gunsmith instead of a lawman. I'd have married, had children and a home. I'd have walked to work every morning, walked home for lunch, then back again until it was time to come home for dinner. I'd never have shot another man and watched him die."

Richard Bates said nothing. He could see the Gunsmith's face in the moonlight, and he had no doubt that Clint was very, very sincere in what he was saying. But Clint was deluding himself. He was not the kind of a man who would ever have been content to lead a routine life. Maybe he did miss a family and home, but not enough to go to the same job every day for twenty or thirty years and do the same boring work.

Clint looked at his sidekick. "You're young and hand-some. Ambitious and intelligent. Why did you come down to Texas? To this? I'm sure you could have remained in the

Midwest and sold farmers and sodbusters all the wire that your manufacturer could produce. Why Texas?"

Richard shrugged his shoulders. "I guess because Mr. Glidden said it was the last place in the world where a man could sell barbed wire. I sort of took that to be a challenge. I wanted to prove myself. And look where I am now."

"You're all right. You have over twenty thousand dollars in cash and you've proven barbed wire can stop charging longhorns. I'd say you've done plenty already."

"I've gotten an old man killed," Richard said tightly. "And I've almost gotten us hung."

Clint could hear the bitterness in Richard's voice. "We'll set things straight before you sell a few spools of wire in Texas and prove your point and then go home, marry, settle down."

"How do you know that's what I'll do?"

"Just a hunch," the Gunsmith said. "I just have a hunch you've a pretty little filly waiting for you back in De Kalb."

For the first time in days, Richard Bates cracked a smile. "You're not only a fast man with a gun, but you're a mind reader. I do have a girl in mind."

"Then I'll have to work all the harder to keep you alive in Texas," Clint said as they rode on into the night.

"You can try, but I'm going to order more wire at the first town we come to. And I'll sell every foot of it this time or die trying."

Clint knew that Richard Bates meant what he said. It was a challenge they both faced. Richard selling his damned barbed wire, Clint keeping the man alive to sell however much wire he needed to sell in order to have proven his point to Glidden.

Chapter Fifteen

With morning came an acute attack of hunger. Clint realized that he had not eaten in over twenty-four hours and his stomach was growling. Richard felt just as bad. The pounding he'd received while tied across a saddle coupled with the beating he'd taken in San Antonio had finally exacted their toll. He clung to the saddlehorn and swayed to the motion of his horse like he was drunk. Clint watched the man carefully, sure that he would topple from the saddle if they did not find a place to rest before midmorning.

"There!" he said to himself as they came over a ridge and stood looking down at what appeared to be a homestead. Clint could see a big field of stunted yellow corn that was clearly suffering from lack of water. A small log cabin stood leaning to the west as if it were about to topple. Smoke drifted up from a rock chimney. Close by was an equally rickety barn and a set of corrals that didn't look as if they could contain milk cows, much less the four thin horses that were milling around inside.

Suddenly, a man and a woman emerged from the cabin. The woman had a bucket in her hand, and she went to a small stream not far from the house. She bent and filled the bucket and straightened, sloshing water on the ground. Clint watched her walk nearly a hundred yards over to the corn and pour the water into a furrow where it was swallowed up by the dry earth almost before it had run past more than a few stalks of corn. Even at a distance, the gesture was so pathetic that it made the Gunsmith frown.

No wonder the corn field was dying! It seemed possible to Clint that a slight rise of ground between the stream and the cornfield could be crossed with a trench thereby eliminating the drudgery of trying to irrigate the corn a single bucket at a time.

Clint watched the woman go after another bucketful of water and, this time, she gave it to a milk cow that stood tied to the end of a rope. Clint could count every one of the cow's ribs. This family looked as if it were on the verge of being starved out of the valley. Clint had seen a lot of poor farms and ranches, but this one was one of the worst. There weren't even any chickens, a sure sign that they had all been butchered and eaten.

The man had gone to the corral and now he was trying to rope one of the horses, but he was having no visible success. After about ten throws, he hung the rope up over a fencepost and headed back to the house. Every line of his body spelled defeat.

"He can't rope," Clint said. "He just flat cannot throw a good ketch rope."

Richard Bates opened his swollen eyes and focused on the scene below. "You think we can buy us a good breakfast for twenty thousand dollars?" he asked weakly. "I'm willing to pay almost that much for food."

"I wouldn't count on much," Clint said dubiously. "This is a mighty poor-looking spread. Don't look like the man is much use for anything. He can't rope, and he sure hasn't been spending much time on repairs. His woman has to try and irrigate that whole damn field with a wooden bucket, and it's obvious that she's failing. So what they have is no corn, no feed for the milk cow, a hen house but no chickens.

That means they have no milk, no eggs, and no broke horses."

Richard said, "But do they have some salt pork or a side of beef or anything to eat?"

"Why don't we find out," Clint suggested. "Maybe things aren't quite as grim as they appear. At least there's smoke coming from the fireplace. That must mean they're cooking something."

Richard did not need any urging. They headed down into the valley. When still a mile away, the woman with the bucket happened to catch sight of them. She straightened up from the furrow and shaded her eyes.

"She sees us," Richard said as they trotted forward. "Pretty-looking from here."

Clint was just about to agree when the woman dropped her bucket and went racing toward the house as if her skirts were on fire.

"Looks like she's the spooky kind," Clint observed.

A moment later, the woman and the man both emerged with rifles. Before Clint could wave or even shout a hello, they opened fire. Richard wheeled his horse around and retreated, still clinging to the saddlehorn. Clint held Duke steady.

"The man can't rope, fix fence, or even shoot a rifle," Clint said with a shake of his head. He had been shot at enough in his life to know when a marksman was getting his range. In this case, not only were the pair off target, they were shooting far too low to allow for the drop of their rifle slugs. Clint could see the bullets hitting the earth a good fifty yards ahead of him.

He waited patiently, secure in the knowledge that he was safe, if they were both aiming at him. And after several minutes and about twenty wasted bullets, the pair stopped firing. When the echoing gunfire rolled away, Clint cupped his hands before his mouth and shouted, "We're friendly and in need of food. We'll pay . . . five dollars for something to eat."

The man and the woman lowered their rifles, and Clint waited while they obviously discussed his offer. The man took off his hat and used it to beat the dust off his pants. It was then that Clint realized that the "man" was really a woman dressed in men's clothing. A woman with yellow hair just like the other one.

Clint scowled. He'd met some women born and raised on ranches who could outride, outrope, and outshoot most men. But this pair obviously did not fit into that category. So what in the hell were they doing out in this country without men to protect them?

Clint looked back over his shoulder at Richard, who had retreated nearly a quarter of a mile. "Come on," he hollered. "Let's see if they at least know how to cook."

Clint rode straight ahead, but when he came to within a hundred yards of the pair, the one wearing men's clothes raised her rifle and shouted, "That's far enough, Mister!"

Clint reined Duke up. "We're hungry, ladies."

"Who are you?"

Clint gave them his name and that of Richard Bates. He explained that they had come from San Antonio.

The one wearing the dress was named Margaret, and Clint could see that she was about twenty years old. Her sister was just a few years her senior and she was named Priscilla. Both were pretty if you liked that windtossed look; sunburned noses, and a few freckles. They were big, strong-looking girls but a little on the thin side, like their poor old milk cow.

Priscilla, being the oldest, seemed to be the one in charge. "You don't work for Matt Timberman, do you?"

"Who is he?"

"I'll ask the questions," Priscilla said, gripping her rifle tightly.

Clint thumbed back his Stetson, hearing his stomach growl. "No, ma'am. I don't even know the man. Like I said, we're from San Antonio. Just passing through."

"What's wrong with him?" Margaret asked, motioning to Richard, who looked pale and unwell.

"He's been beaten by some men."

Priscilla said, "Both of you got nasty-looking necks. You escape from a hanging or something?"

"A lynching we did not deserve," the Gunsmith told her. "Ma'am, we're hungry and tired. We have money to pay for food and a place to rest. Then we'll be moving on."

"You said five dollars for a breakfast," Priscilla said. "You mean that?"

"I did."

Priscilla lowered her rifle. She had high, broad cheekbones, pale blue eyes, and fair skin. She and her sister both looked Scandanavian, and Clint could detect a faint Swedish accent. "Mister, to be honest, I haven't seen that much money in a long time."

"We could buy a used plow, maybe," Margaret said hopefully. "And a harness for the horses."

Priscilla nodded. "If I could catch one to harness." She looked at Clint with sudden interest. "Mister, can you rope?"

"A little," he said, "but I never claimed to be a cowboy."

"What are you?"

"A gunsmith."

She lowered the rifle but did not put it down, and her voice was laced with skepticism. "You don't look like any gunsmith or businessman to me."

Clint tried to curb his impatience. "Listen," he said in

his most reasonable voice, "we just need something to eat."

"Let's see your money."

Clint started to reach into the pocket of his jeans but realized that he had no money. He stepped back to his saddlebags, and even though Bert had taken ten thousand, they were still crammed with greenbacks. He felt a little ridiculous reaching into the bags and pulling out a fistful of currency, then discovering that the smallest denomination was a fifty-dollar bill.

"Hang on," he said, "there must be something smaller in here. Ahh, here we go. A ten."

The two women were speechless. Priscilla raised her rifle and shouted, "Hands up. You're bank robbers?"

Clint raised his hands quickly because, at this close range, even this woman could probably blow a hole in his chest.

Margaret quickly covered Richard, who stared at her for a moment, and then just passed out and tumbled from his horse to land in the dirt.

"What's wrong with him?" Margaret cried. "Has he been shot?"

"No," Clint said, his voice filling with anger. "He probably just died of hunger, and you can both consider yourselves guilty of murder!"

"We are not!" Priscilla argued. "You must be bank robbers. How else could you have so much money?"

Clint had been pushed as far as he could go. Without answering, he dropped his reins and stepped up to Priscilla. He grabbed the barrel of the rifle and twisted the weapon out of her hand, at the same time knocking Margaret down and taking her rifle.

Priscilla yelped in anger and threw herself at Clint. She hit him with closed fists, and she was strong. He rocked back on his heels and just managed to duck a second punch.

When Priscilla lost her balance, Clint gave her a swift kick in the backside that dumped her unceremoniously to the dirt.

"We'll pay you ten whole dollars for breakfast if you can add something in a sack for us to take down the trail," he said exasperatedly.

"How much is the reward on your heads?" Priscilla said, her eyes going from Clint to Richard, then back again.

Clint had had enough. He started for the cabin, figuring to grab whatever food he could before loading up Richard, paying these two fool sisters, and riding out of here.

"Where do you think you're going?" Priscilla cried as she hurried after him.

Clint pushed the door open and stomped into the cabin. It was neat and very clean. But when he got to the cupboards, he discovered that, except for a few spices, the cabin was empty of food. Clint saw a pile of chewed corncobs by the door. They were runty little things, not three inches long. It hit him all at once that the sisters were also probably starving to death. There wasn't a crumb of bread or a piece of beef, venison, or pork to be had on the entire ranch.

Priscilla stood beside the door and watched Clint as he opened one empty cupboard after another and then inspected the empty flour barrel. "As you can see, we have nothing but the old milk cow. If you will pay us ten dollars, I will try and butcher her. There would be enough meat to fry and then take with you."

"I don't want to eat that damned, skinny, tough old cow!" Clint pitched the woman's Winchester onto a tick mattress. He took a deep breath and fought to control his hunger. "All right, why are you two women out here starving to death?"

"This is our home," Priscilla said.

"Where are your men?"

"Dead," she told him. "They were killed by either the Comanche or by Matt Timberman and his men early this spring."

"Couldn't tell the difference between an Indian's killing and that of a white man?" Clint asked, finding it difficult to believe this woman was telling the truth.

But Priscilla shook her head, and her face suddenly looked pinched. "By the time we found the bodies, they were both beyond recognizing. They'd been shot and then tied behind their horses. The horses had dragged them over . . . over rocks. If . . . if it hadn't been for my husband's wedding band. . . ."

Priscilla crumpled in the doorway and wept. Clint expelled a deep breath. He had been wrong. His bad luck was still holding. Now, instead of just having Richard Bates to look after, he also had two sisters!

"We'll take you to a town," he said quietly. "We'll even leave you some money to get a new start."

She looked up at him, her pale blue eyes red and angry. "No! This valley is ours! Our husbands were brothers. They homesteaded it together before they sent for us."

"Sent for you from where?"

Priscilla said, "From Minnesota. We were . . . we were mail-order brides."

"I see." Clint scratched his head. "Can't you go back to where you came from? You must have families. Someone who can take care of you in Minnesota."

"No. We stay. This ranch is very valuable. That's why Mr. Timberman wants it. He uses our water, and he drives his cattle into our corn fields. He has offered us three hundred dollars for this valley."

"Maybe you ought to take it. That's three or four times what you'll need to reach Minnesota."

She shook her head and raised her chin. "This is good land. We stay."

"How can you stay? You haven't got a corn crop. It's starting to die. And those four horses in the corral aren't worth much. You have no food, no money. . . ."

Priscilla turned around. "I will kill the cow and then we will have ten dollars."

She started to go, but Clint grabbed her arm. "Wait a minute. You need a milk cow. Besides, the meat would be tougher than shoe leather."

"It is all we have."

Clint expelled a breath. "Any deer around these parts?"

"Yes. But we never hit them when we shoot."

"Doesn't surprise me at all." Clint placed his hand on her shoulder. "I'll hunt up a deer. In the meantime, try and make some broth for my friend. Bandage and clean him up. He's a good man."

Priscilla nodded. "Is he a gunsmith, too?"

"No." Clint said. "He's a barbed wire salesman."

"A what?"

"Never mind," Clint said as he started for his horse. "With luck, we'll have venison for supper. You can butcher and cook meat, can't you?"

She nodded and, for the first time, even smiled. The smile transformed her features, and she looked almost girlishly pretty. "You bring us meat, we cook it good."

Clint was relieved. He didn't mind shooting a deer for meat when he was hungry, but he had never liked butchering the things. At least these two sisters were not completely worthless. But one thing was sure, he needed to talk them into leaving this ranch. They were no match for the elements here, let alone this Timberman fellow and whatever Comanche might still prowl in these parts looking for easy pickings. Young white women sold for a hundred dollars a head down in Mexico. The Comancheros had been dealing in slaves for over a hundred years, and it was profitable business.

Clint wondered if Priscilla and Margaret even suspected how dangerous it was for two pretty women to be alone on the frontier. Especially if they were not skilled in ranch work and could not shoot straight.

He would have to tell them. But it could wait until after supper.

Chapter Sixteen

Clint wiped the grime and sweat from his face before he gripped the plow handles in his fists. He looked to Richard and said, "Duke has never pulled a plow blade, but if you and Margaret will walk on either side of him and talk gentle, then I think he'll consent to this monumental indignity."

Richard and Margaret each took ahold of Duke's bridle and began talking to the horse.

"Let's go," Clint said, feeling the harness snap taut as the plow bit into the earth. The harness was makeshift, but it was strong. The plow that they had bought in the small town of Bandolier was badly worn but serviceable. If they could just cut a deep and wide enough canal through the rise of land to drain water from the stream into the field, they could turn everything around on this hard-scrabble ranch.

Duke threw his muscle into the harness, and the plow sank deep into the rich soil. Its shiny blade cut smoothly and then, as the powerful gelding pulled and strained, the plow sliced forward, turning the sod so that roots and earthworms were sticking up at the sun.

"Keep him moving!" Clint shouted, as the plow struck an underground rock. The jarring deflection almost hurled the Gunsmith to his knees. "Don't let him stop!"

The muscles in Clint's arms bulged with tension, and he

gritted his teeth as he leaned on the plow handles and willed them to stay down so that the blade would continue to turn the heavy soil. Fifty feet, then a hundred, and then all the way through the rise of land and right up to the edge to the withered cornfield. By the time they'd finished, Clint was sopping wet with effort, and even Duke was trembling with exertion.

But Priscilla hugged his neck and mopped the sweat from his brow. "Clint, it isn't the straightest furrow in the world, but it's deep and it's a start. The first one ought to be the hardest. Let me take the second."

"Uh-uh," Clint said. Priscilla was strong for a woman, but not strong enough to make another cut. "Richard can take the second pass back to the stream. You and Margaret can have the third and the fourth. After that, I'm afraid it's mostly going to be pick and shovel work."

"Margaret and I can do that while you and Richard set fence posts and string that new barbed wire."

"Sounds like you girls have it all planned out."

In the few weeks that Clint and Richard had been staying at this ranch, the four of them had grown close. Clint had initially just wanted to stay a short while while he taught Richard how to handle a gun, but there was so much work to be done here that they had just decided to stay and turn things around for these two sisters. Clint had broken the four thin horses, cut some grass for the cow, and then Richard had ordered and received a new shipment of barbed wire, which they'd stored in the barn along with the other things they'd bought. During the day, they worked so hard that they slept well at night, the women in their cabin, he and Richard in the barn—after all, the sisters were recently widowed and, therefore, not to be trifled with out of feelings of lust.

Between work and sleep, Clint made sure that for one

hour every morning and evening they had shooting lessons and practice. Richard Bates had proven that he had excellent hand speed and a real knack for drawing and firing. Had he wanted to be a gunfighter, he could have held his own if he'd lived through his inexperience. The women were also very coordinated and, given their troubles with Matt Timberman, were more than eager to learn how to defend their interests.

"He'll be coming one day," Priscilla warned. "He and his riders will come just as soon as he realizes we're going to be able to irrigate our corn."

Clint had no reason not to believe the woman. Besides, quite often during the day when he and Richard were working, he'd see riders silently watching them. Sometimes they'd watch for hours before disappearing back into the forest. Priscilla swore that they were Timberman's men, but Clint had no way of knowing if this was true or not. Still, when men watched and then vanished in silence, their actions caused a sense of foreboding that could not be easily dismissed.

"If this Timberman fella is looking for trouble. I wish he'd come and get it started."

"He's smarter than that," Priscilla said. "He knows that time is on his side. All he has to do is wait until the water is ready to flow to the corn and then he'll come."

"Let him," Clint said in a flat, emotionless voice. "We'll be waiting. Besides, you'll be able to shoot a whole lot straighter."

Priscilla wanted to change the subject. She closed one blue eye and peered down the freshly plowed row Clint had made. "It appears to me that you're a natural-born farmer," she teased. "You handled that plow like you were born to do it all your life."

"The hell I was," Clint said with a smile.

The Gunsmith waited until Duke had stopped trembling, then he let Richard take the plow handles, and they turned the implement around and started back to the stream. The second cut was much easier. Priscilla had her turn and, this time, they kept the plow down in the furrow they'd made from the first two passes. The idea was to simply deepen the furrow and keep deepening it until it acted like a canal and delivered water to the thirsty cornfield.

At noon, they stopped, and Clint unhitched Duke, then hitched Richard's horse to the plow. The palomino did not like the idea, but after he realized he had no choice in the matter, the animal settled down and pulled steadily all afternoon while Clint and Richard began to dig post holes.

Digging post holes was the hardest, meanest work that either man had ever done. Hour after hour they pounded away with a pick and a shovel. If the soil had been soft and rock-free, they could have dug a hole every ten minutes, but most of the time, they struck a rock and either had to dig it out with a pick, or else start another hole and hope it was easier.

By evening, both Clint and Richard were exhausted, but they looked with no small satisfaction on their work. "Another two, maybe three days and we can sink posts," Clint estimated.

"After we cut them," Richard said, placing his hands on his hips and studying the work yet to be done. "Clint, I'll tell you one thing. I think putting up this fencing will really prove to everyone in this part of the country how valuable barbed wire can be to them. They'll see how we protected this cornfield and they'll buy wire like whiskey."

Clint was no farmer, but as the days got warmer, and despite the fact that they were all working several hours a day to bring water in bucketfulls to the corn, even he could tell it wasn't going to last much longer. "If we don't get that canal to these fields in a couple of days, there won't be any corn to save."

"I know," Richard said in agreement. "There's nearly a full moon tonight, maybe we should work right on through. Be a little cooler."

"That's a good idea," Clint said. "Those two women are the hardest workers I ever saw in my life. They'll work themselves into an early grave if they don't slow down."

"They'll slow down when we get the water to this poor cornfield and have this fence up. After that, we can all take things easier." Richard reached down and picked up some soil. He rubbed it between his thumb and forefinger, studying it closely. "Clint, my father was a farmer."

Clint leaned on his pick. "Is that right?"

"Yep. We planted corn and harvested it every year. It was a much shorter growing season up where I come from, but we had better rains. Clint?"

"What?"

"I'm glad we stayed to help these women. That Margaret is pretty special."

"So is her sister," Clint said, guessing that Richard was already beginning to forget his sweetheart back in Illinois. It happened a lot. Out of sight, out of mind was more than just a clever saying. It was true that Richard was spending more and more time with Margaret. When he wasn't actually working beside her, he was watching her.

"Clint, have you and Priscilla . . . well . . ."

Clint frowned. "Well, what?"

"You know." Richard's cheeks colored.

"No," Clint said.

"Oh. Margaret and I are sort of . . . attached."

"Attached how?" Clint asked.

"Well, we think a lot of each other. And . . . " Richard toed the earth. "Well, I was just wondering what you thought of her."

"I like her. She's pretty, but they both work too hard. Working out in the fields will age a woman fast."

"They need husbands."

Now Clint understood. "Listen," he said. "I know they need husbands. But don't start thinking about me in terms of being one of them. If you want to marry the girl and farm this valley, that's one thing. But I'm not ready to settle down."

"Well, me neither!" Richard's feelings had been hurt and his pride stung. "I just was thinking that if we ever were ready to settle, this wouldn't be such a bad deal."

"By then," Clint said, "we'll both be old, fat, gray-haired, and potbellied—if we aren't dead. You're thinking too much, Richard. What about your dream of fencing the West? Have you already let a woman turn you away from your life's work?"

"Of course not! Let's get busy."

Clint looked up at the sun diving into the western horizon. He had angered Richard and that was probably necessary for his own well-being. The two sisters would find themselves two good farmers and raise a brood of children. That was what they wanted and what they deserved. Clint figured that Richard Bates was a man of some destiny. He was smitten, but that did not mean he should throw all his grand dreams away even before he'd had a chance to try them on for size.

No girl was worth that much.

Chapter Seventeen

They worked on the canal by moonlight. It was cool, and now that the hard surface of the earth had been penetrated by the plow, it was simply a matter of digging out enough dirt to make the water flow from the stream to the field.

Margaret made coffee, lots of it, hot and black, but by midnight, it became apparent that they could not work much longer. Their bodies were weary, and Clint knew that there was no sense in any of them pushing themselves to the point of total exhaustion.

So they sat on the withered grass and drank the good, black coffee, each lost in his or her own thoughts. After a little while, Margaret and Richard walked off toward the cabin, leaving Clint and Priscilla alone in the moonlight.

"Clint?" Her voice sounded a little sad.

He was close enough to smell her. She smelled earthy, and Clint knew that if he touched her earlobe with his tongue, it would taste salty. "What is it, Priscilla?"

"I don't know what to say to my sister. I'm afraid she's fallen in love with Richard."

Clint let her go on without offering any comment.

"I like him, but he's leaving, isn't he?"

"I think so."

"I'm sure of it," Priscilla whispered sadly. "I just don't want to see Margaret get hurt again. I mean, she didn't love her husband, not did I mine. We were mail-order brides, and the brothers were not . . . well, particularly affectionate or kind. They were good men, but they treated us like property. We still felt terrible when they were killed. But I'll be honest, part of our grief was just born of simple fear for ourselves."

"A woman alone out here is pretty fair game for outlaws and Indians," Clint said, wondering if he should tell her about the Comancheros. He decided she had enough to worry about for the moment.

Priscilla turned around and looked toward the cabin. "My little sister admitted that she knows Richard. I mean, *really* knows him. Clint, what if she comes up with child?"

"I guess he'd marry her," Clint said.

"A woman out here with a baby . . . I just don't know what would happen."

"You'd make do. Life goes on." Clint knew that his words were not as comforting as Priscilla might have liked to hear, but they were true. "Maybe if she had a child, they'd get married. And maybe you'd sell this place and go to a town."

"We come from a town," Priscilla said, turning back to look at the Gunsmith. "A pretty town. I was always more like a mother than an older sister to Margaret. Our own mother died when we were young. Our father wasn't much."

Clint rolled over and gripped the woman's shoulders. "You said when Margaret was little. She isn't little or a girl anymore, Priscilla. Your baby sister has become a woman, one already once married. She's old enough to decide what she wants to do with her life, and her . . . her body. Let it be."

She folded into his arms. "I hope you are right. I've been so wanting to hear you say that it was all right."

"What's all right?"

Priscilla kissed him full on the mouth. "That I behave like Margaret and know you, Clint. That we make love until you decide to leave this country."

"Is that what you want?"

"More than anything."

He nodded, because despite being as tired as he felt, it was what he wanted, too. Clint took her into his arms. The night was warm, the stars seemed very close.

"I should go to the stream and take a bath," she whispered. "I must smell terrible."

"If you smelled clean then you'd know how dirty I smelled," Clint said. "We've been working like farm animals, Priscilla. What we smell like or whether or not we have dirt under our fingernails or between our toes doesn't matter."

Clint sat up. He unbuttoned her man's shirt and then untied the rope that served as a belt. Priscilla shrugged out of her own dirty clothes, spread them on the withered grass, and then lay down upon them. The moonlight made her skin glow. Her eyes were closed, her lips slightly parted. "I been having a fever for you since the day I first saw you."

"Open your eyes," Clint said as he peeled off his shirt and yanked off his boots. He stood up and unbuckled the gunbelt he wore. He set it down very carefully beside her and then unbuttoned his pants. She watched, and he noticed that her breathing was already starting to quicken. Clint stepped out of his pants, and his manhood stood straight out from his lean, weary, but suddenly very eager body.

"Oh my," Priscilla whispered. "It's so big. My husband . . ."

She suddenly realized what she was saying, even as she spread her strong legs and reached up for him. "Come inside of me," she begged.

Clint dropped to his knees between her legs. It was amazing how a man could suddenly find life in his weary body given the sight of a man-hungry woman. He bent and took one of her nipples in his mouth. Her breasts were large and incredibly soft. Large-bosomed and wide in the hips, Priscilla and her sister were built for a man to get energetic upon.

"Yep," he said. "You do taste salty from honest sweat."

Priscilla giggled. "I told you I needed a bath."

"And I told you I wanted to make love to a sweaty, smelly woman tonight," he said, sucking on her nipple and feeling it harden.

She grabbed his manhood and pulled on it. Her generous hips arched upward and she made a soft, moaning sound in her throat. "Then do it, Clint. Make love to me now!"

Clint decided that there was neither the need for foreplay, nor did either of them have the extra strength for it. So he let her guide him into her. She was surprisingly tight, but when she raised her knees, he rolled his hips forward, and he felt himself slip in all the way.

"Oh, yes!" she groaned. Her hips began to bounce up and down. "Come on, Clint! I know you know how to pleasure a woman!"

Clint raised his head. At that very moment, he heard Margaret cry out in ecstasy from the cabin, and he knew that Richard also knew how to pleasure a woman. Clint began to drive himself in and out of Priscilla, and she dug her fingernails into his buttocks when he started to rotate them in a slow but powerful ellipsis.

"Don't torture me, Clint," she pleaded. "I can't stand it if you do that."

Clint changed the direction of the rotation, and she began to toss her head back and forth as her body jerked up and down trying to meet his with greater and greater force. They were slick with sweat now, and their bodies made wet, sucking sounds as they slammed against each other. Clint could feel Priscilla coming faster and faster.

Suddenly, she stiffened and cried, "Oh, yes! Ohhhh! Yes!"

Clint covered her mouth with his own as his penis propelled itself into the wet cavern of her womanhood and began to spew his seed in great spurts. He emptied himself in drenching torrents as the woman cried silently.

When the blood stopped pounding in his ears and their bodies stopped spasming together, Clint rolled off the woman and stared up at the stars. That was when he heard Margaret and Richard giggling.

"They must have heard you," he said to the woman who lay gasping beside him.

Priscilla managed to gulp and say, "I'll bet they heard me in San Antonio. I never had a man that could do that to me."

She rolled over on one elbow and looked at this face. "Would you do it once more? Please?"

Clint groaned. He needed sleep, but a gentleman just did not refuse a lady.

Chapter Eighteen

"What you have to do," Clint explained, "is to let the palm of your hand slap the butt of your six-gun and then bring it up smoothly, cocking back the hammer so that when the barrel is pointed at your target, you're ready to fire."

"That's what I've been doing," Richard said. "I've been doing it for the last four weeks! I still can't draw and fire half as fast as you."

"Neither could a hell of a lot of professional gunfighters," Clint said a little impatiently. "The thing of it is, you'll never be a gunfighter. You don't want to be a gunfighter. All you are trying to do is to be able to draw and fire with speed and—above all—accuracy. Now, let's see you do it again."

Clint stood back. Richard had the ability, but he lacked concentration and patience. A man who had never used guns until the age of twenty-four would probably never be the equal of a man who had grown up with a squirrel rifle in his hands. Richard wanted things too fast. And then, too, he was working too hard in the daytime and playing with Margaret half the night. There were dark circles under his eyes, and if it wasn't for the fact that these two sisters obviously needed help, they would have been better off leaving this valley.

Richard bent slightly at the knees. His hand hovered over

his gunbutt, and then it darted down and hit the walnut handle of his Navy Colt. The gun came up too fast, and when it was leveled, Richard was still trying to cock the hammer back so that he could fire. It was a mess of a draw, and Richard was furious with himself. "Dammit! I was doing better last week!"

"That's right," Clint said. "You were. Last week, you were listening to me and not rushing it so hard. So go slower this time and try to hit the fence post."

"You can do it," Margaret said.

Clint frowned. He was having enough trouble getting Richard to concentrate on the draw and firing of his gun without having a pretty young woman to compete with. "Margaret, please go back to work. You've had your shooting practice, and I just need a few minutes more with Richard."

The girl blew Richard a kiss and walked back to the canal, which was almost finished. Clint noticed how Margaret made sure to sway her hips provocatively, as if to tell Clint that he could not possibly compete for Richard's attentions against her womanly charms. And she was right.

"Okay, Richard, slow it down and concentrate on the shooting part," Clint said. "The fastest man with the gun isn't the one that wins gunfights. It's the man who can be quick and who shoots straightest."

Richard shoved the Navy back in its holster. "That's what you keep saying."

"Then remember it! Now draw and make it smooth and easy. Shoot from the hip, but do it with some thought."

Clint had Richard standing twenty feet from a fence post. The post was half the diameter of most men, and fifteen feet was farther than most gunfights took place. If Richard could draw and fire with some speed and hit that post three times out of four, he would be better than most men with a six-gun.

Richard drew, and he concentrated on a single, continuous, and very smooth motion. The gun came up in his fist even as he thumbed back the hammer. As soon as the Navy was level and pointed, he squeezed rather than jerked the trigger. To his amazement, the bullet hit the post and splinters of wood flew everywhere. He had never done it so well before. Not the drawing and the shooting together.

"Excellent!" Clint said, genuinely pleased. "When you put your mind to it, you've come a long, long way in just a few weeks."

Richard grinned, knowing it was true. The Gunsmith was a tough and demanding teacher, but all that he asked was concentration and dedication. He didn't expect superior quickness or reflexes, just that a man did the best with his abilities.

"Now," Clint said, "reholster and walk back ten paces. Draw quickly and raise your gun to eye level. As soon as your eye, the barrel, and the front sight of that gun are all level and on line, then squeeze off your shot. Don't hurry, but don't hesitate. If you think a split second longer than is necessary, you'll either be dead or you'll mess up your shot."

Richard did as he was told. He fired and missed, but he had the feeling that he had been close.

"Again," Clint said. "And don't think! Just act."

"It's hard not to think," Richard said.

"What's to think about when you face a man?" Clint drew and fired, his own gun bucking twice in his hand and the shots so close together that they sounded like one continuous roll of thunder.

He reloaded and reholstered. "If you're too busy thinking

at a time when you should be acting, you'll fail. Your mind will be divided between thoughts of how to survive, and what it should be doing. Just blank your mind and let your reflexes and body do the work they have to do. Believe me, Richard, after you shoot a man, you'll have plenty of time to do more than enough thinking."

Richard nodded. "Yeah. I never killed a man before. I don't want to in the future. But I might not have any choice. Right?"

"Right. Now try again."

This time, Richard did it the way he was supposed to. He took a fraction of a second and, with his gun extended at arm's length, he aimed and fired. It all worked, and the post took another slug.

"Good!" Clint said. "You've got the basics, all you need to do is practice."

"What about Margaret and Priscilla?"

Clint was not exactly sure what Richard meant, but he said, "They have improved a great deal with their Winchesters. If I let them shoot at me today from the same distance they did when we first saw them, they'd nail me."

"That's not what I meant," Richard said. "I mean, what are we going to do about them?"

"We're going to cut about a thousand posts and then string wire around their cornfield," Clint said. "Just as soon as we finish up the canal today."

Richard grinned. "Yeah," he said. "Today we do it."

With that, they went to work. The canal was shallow where it left the stream and also where it entered the corn field. But they'd had to dig down almost five feet to cut through the rise of land. That had been the tough part, but it was finished now. They were ready to open the dike at the stream and let the water flow.

Priscilla and Margaret were as excited as children. Clint and Richard gave them the honor of digging out the dike and letting the rush of water come racing into their new canal. They raced along the canal, following the water like four kids.

"There it goes!" Richard shouted, as the foaming water slowed a little but passed through the rise of land and then hurried down toward the thirsty field of corn.

When the water gurgled into the cornfield, they all let out a holler of joy. They hugged each other and danced around and around. It was a beautiful sight to watch the life-giving water surge across the cornfield. It was such a small thing, but for some reason, Clint knew that gutting it out and finishing this damned canal would always remain one of the most satisfying accomplishments of his lifetime. They had worked like dogs for weeks, and this was the payoff. Oh, sure, the cornfield was already stunted, but it would come back some. And next year . . . next year and the corn in this field would grow six feet tall.

They celebrated by taking the afternoon off. It was a warm summer day, and they followed the stream for almost a mile until they came to a place where there was a deep swimming hole. None of them had anything to swim in except their birthday suits but, after a few timid moments by the women, that went just fine, too. Margaret and Priscilla were built exactly alike and seeing the body of one without clothes was just like seeing the body of the other.

They swam and frolicked for nearly two hours. They washed their dirt-caked clothes on the rocks and dried them on bushes. It was great fun and when Richard took Margaret's hand and led her upstream, Clint pulled Priscilla down in the clean sand and rode her with such skill that she climaxed three times before he satisfied himself.

Clint said, "Both you and your sister looked like girls when that water came rushing through the canal this morning."

"I felt like a girl then," Priscilla said. "But lying next to you, I sure feel every inch a woman."

Clint laughed. "I think we had better get on back to the cabin and make sure we aren't flooding the cornfield. After irrigating it with a bucket for so long, it might drown."

But she clung to him a moment later. She wrapped her arms around his neck and her legs around his hips. "Are you going away now that the canal is finished?" she whispered.

"No. There's that barbed wire fence to put up yet."

"But you will go soon." It was not a question. He had told her from the very beginning that he could never be a homesteader and that he had a lust to wander.

"You've always known that I would."

"Yes."

Clint took a deep breath and wiggled his hips so that she giggled and gave him a pull with the muscles inside of her. "I won't hurry off," he promised. "I won't go until it's safe for you and your sister."

Priscilla squeezed him with her whole body. "If I could hold you in me like this forever, that is exactly what I'd do."

"Then the corn would drown for sure."

"To hell with the corn!" She giggled. "What does a woman need corn for when she is holding a man like you inside of her?"

Clint didn't know. It was a very good question.

Chapter Nineteen

Clint swung the axe, feeling it bite into the small pine tree. He swung a half dozen more times and then the tree fell. It was only about as big around as his thigh and less than fifteen feet tall. Clint used his axe to trim the branches off the trunk. He cut the tree in half and had two more fence posts ready to load in the wagon.

His hands had long since blistered and formed calluses because of the heavy shovel work and the post hole digging he'd accomplished during the past month. His back no longer ached, and he felt stronger than he had in years. Hell, he thought, a man has to be in better shape working outdoors every day than he would be sleeping until noon and then sitting at a desk or in front of a poker table in some smoky saloon.

Still, the Gunsmith had about had his fill of playing the farmer and rancher. He wasn't afraid of hard physical work, but there were a lot of other things that were more enjoyable, and nobody lived forever. So they'd put in the barbed wire fence and then maybe pay a visit to this Matt Timberman fella and get him straightened out real quick. After that, Clint was thinking about Austin and Anita. Priscilla was plumb wearing him down to the bone. He needed to get away from her before both the woman and her damned black soil got so deep into his pores he could not get rid of either one.

"Hey, Clint!"

The Gunsmith looked over toward Richard. "Yeah?"

"Watch this!"

With real speed of hand, Richard spun and drew his Colt, then fired from the hip. His bullet smashed a pinecone from its branch. "How did you like that!"

"Do it once more," Clint said, "and I'll tell you."

Richard looked disappointed. But he holstered his gun. Turned around and then spun and drew a second time. Again, his shot was perfect and another pinecone exploded from the tree.

"Well?"

"Once more," Clint said, enjoying the look of exasperation that crossed the young Midwesterner's begrimed face.

"Well, dammit, Clint!" Richard cried. But he turned around anyway. Set himself, then spun and fired. This time, the bullet missed its mark.

Clint nodded his head up and down. "You're sure getting there. Two out of three times shooting that quick is pretty good by most anyone's standards."

"But not yours," Richard said almost petulantly.

"It takes time." Clint studied the pile of posts they had cut so far this day. He glanced up at the sun and saw that it was late afternoon. "I guess if we load up what we've cut, we'll have done enough work for today."

"Suits me," Richard said, shoving his gun back into his holster.

"Reload," Clint instructed in a flat, uncompromising voice. "Don't ever put a half-empty gun back in your holster. Always reload while it's in your fist. That way, if all of a sudden you find yourself in a shooting scrape, you got six beans in the barrel ready to fire."

"I thought gunfighters always rode with their hammer on an empty cylinder."

"Nope," Clint said. "A lot of cowboys do, though. They're working on horseback, and they take spills. But a professional gunman isn't nearly as worried about dropping his gun or taking a spill and having an accidental shot as he is running out of bullets in a sudden fight. I keep six in mine, and you can do the same or not. Doesn't matter to me. You have to decide."

Richard yanked his gun out and reloaded. He had been told that lesson about fifty times, but he still forgot and that annoyed Clint.

"I may decide to stay awhile after the fence is up," Richard said without looking at Clint.

"Do as you want," Clint said. "It's a free country."

"That's right." It was plain by his voice that Richard was irritated. "What the devil is so important that you have to go away for?"

"Nothing to brag about," Clint said. "It's just that I like to move around some. See new places and people."

"New women is what you mean."

"New women are important, too," Clint admitted.

"You're going to break Priscilla's heart when you go. You know that, don't you, Clint?"

"She'll cry," he said. "They do sometimes, but a man has to ask himself which is the better?"

"The better of what?"

Clint pushed his sweat-stained Stetson back on his head. "Which is the better—a man born to travel getting stuck in one place and finding himself mad and bitter over it—or a man realizing he has limitations to how much responsibility he wants and then walking away before he messes up a good woman with children he don't want or isn't willing to raise."

Clint didn't figure to preach, but Richard needed to think about some things if he was considering planting his roots in this country. "If a man gets married and settles in, I figure he better be man enough to raise his kids right up to their own manhood. Either that, or not have any in the first place."

"It's not as simple as that," Richard said after a few minutes. "Men and women change. Everything changes."

"Responsibility and right and wrong don't change," Clint said stubbornly. "But then, I guess I'm old-fashioned in the way I think. It's my own code I live by, and every man has to answer to his own conscience. God knows I have enough to answer for ten men."

"You're one of the best men I ever met," Richard said point-blank. "You saved my life in San Antonio, and you did it out of principle, not for your own gain. And you're here because of the same reasons."

Clint chuckled. "I'm having fun working hard. But the novelty is about to wear off soon enough. Priscilla will find another man. A man better for her than I could ever be. They'll raise corn and kids and in five years, she won't even remember my face. In ten years, she'll have forgotten my name."

Richard shook his head. "I don't believe a word of that."

"Doesn't matter," Clint said. "Let's get the wagon loaded and get a move on back to the ranch. If we get there in time, we might even have time to set a few posts before dark."

"You and Priscilla have plenty in common," Richard grumbled. "Like the way you work your tails off from dawn to dusk."

"If you and Margaret weren't acting like a couple of damned rabbits half the night, maybe we'd get a little work out of the both of you."

Richard blushed and started loading the posts.

Chapter Twenty

It had taken them longer than they'd expected to load up the freshly cut posts. By the time they had gotten the wagon turned around and headed back to the ranch, it was nearly sunset.

"We won't be setting any posts today," Clint said.

"Good." Richard expelled a weary breath. "I'm tired tonight for some reason. I think I'd better try and get more sleep."

"That helps," Clint said as he drove the wagon and wondered what Priscilla would have cooked for supper. Since coming to work for them, they'd used some of Richard's winnings to buy plenty of supplies. People could not work hard day after day without substantial food to eat. They needed meat and vegetables and coffee and sometimes some dessert. Priscilla and Margaret had started to make some cakes and pies, and that sure did make a man feel like the day's work counted for something.

They were both lost in thought when they crossed over a low ridge and looked down into the valley. The light was fading, but there was still enough of it to see that about a thousand head of cattle were standing in the corn field or milling around in the ranch yard. Clint spotted at least six cowboys hazing a bunch more cattle back and forth across their precious canal in an attempt to collapse its sides and render it useless. There were bound to be a few more cowboys inside the cabin.

Clint lashed the horses into a run. "Hang onto your seat and your gun," he called, "we're about to see how much you've really learned."

The wagon came twisting down the hillside, throwing posts in their wake. Clint did not give a damn. He cussed himself for leaving the two sisters alone while he and Richard had gone to the forest to work.

The cornfield was already half trampled down and the cattle were eating the ears of corn like they were locust. Clint went straight at the cattle and when he got near enough, he began to shout and wave. The cattle looked up quickly, then started to run through the fields.

"Damn them!" Richard shouted.

"It's not them to blame, it's the man who ordered those cowboys to drive the herd into this valley."

"Maybe so, but it's the cowboys we have to worry about right now," Richard said nervously.

Clint pulled the team down to a trot as the cowboys jumped onto their horses and came charging forward with their guns out. "Richard, if they open fire, then we—"

A bullet spun Clint's Stetson right off his head. He dug for his own gun even as Richard fired. The Midwesterner missed, but his bullet must have passed damn close to the lead rider's face because the man jerked his horse sideways so hard the animal spilled into the cornfield.

Clint fired but missed, too. The wagon was jumping three feet into the sky whenever they went over a furrow. It was like sledding across a giant washboard.

"Jump!" Clint yelled.

"But—"

Clint grabbed his young friend by the arm and yanked him right out of his seat. They flew into the air and plowed through about a yard of horseshit and cornstalks before they managed to twist around and face the oncoming riders.

"Hold your gun out and aim before you fire!" Clint yelled, pulling the trigger of his gun and watching a rider flip over the back of his horse.

Richard aimed and his shot was right on target as another empty-saddled horse shied away and raced off to the north.

The other four riders had had enough. They wheeled their horses around and raced for the cabin. Clint winged one of them in the shoulder, but the man hung on and managed to get into the cabin.

Once inside, the cowboys knocked out the two glass windows that were Priscilla and Margaret's pride and joy. They commenced to warm the air with their bullets.

"We're outgunned!" Richard shouted as he pressed his body down into a row of corn.

"That's for sure," Clint said, watching their wagon disappear down the valley. "But we sure had them on the run for a few minutes."

Richard looked at him like he was crazy. "There must be ten of them inside that cabin! Why don't they charge us!"

"Don't give them any foolish ideas," Clint said. "Oh, hell, you just did."

Sure enough, the cowboys came flying out of the cabin. They were smart enough to fan out in a line, but there was no way for them to know they were up against the Gunsmith and his student.

"Shoot 'em in the legs!" Clint shouted.

"The legs?"

"Yeah, that'll take the fight right out of them."

"I never practiced shooting at legs."

Clint demonstrated. He put a bullet right through the fleshy part of a man's thigh, and the poor unfortunate collapsed in a screaming heap. "See, it's easy."

Richard stuck his head above the furrow and then his gun. He aimed, fired, and took a man down. "Hey! Did you see that shot, Clint!"

"Hell, yes! But don't stop!"

They wounded two more before the charge broke, and what remained of the cowboys threw their guns down and their arms up in the air.

"We beat them!" Richard cried. "Two against a dozen and we won!"

Clint had his mind on other things. "I just hope somebody besides myself knows something about doctoring. I won't take any pleasure in seeing those boys bleed to death."

Richard was almost as charitable. Having survived his first major gunbattle, he was feeling very, very fortunate and exhilarated.

"I'll bandage them up. I know something about doctoring because I used to go make housecalls with my Uncle Thurber. He was a country doctor. I used to help him all the time."

"Good," Clint said, getting to his feet and marching ahead with his gun trained on the men. "If any of you think you can catch me by surprise, you had better change your minds. Get their guns, Richard."

Richard was more than happy to do that. When their weapons had been collected, Clint said, "Where are the two women?"

Not one of the cowboys said a word.

Clint looked at Richard. "Shoot each one in the other leg. Best place to cripple them is in the knee."

The cowboys paled even more than they already had. One summed up the feelings of his friends when he said, "You cripple us, we can't earn a living no more."

"The hell with your living!" Clint said angrily. "This homestead belongs to two women and they're gone! Now, either tell me where they are or I'll blow your kneecaps off and we'll ride away hearing your screams."

To put emphasis to his words, Clint put a bullet through one of the cowboy's pantslegs. The shot was intended to just pluck at the cloth, but it must have been a hair off because the man howled and grabbed his knee. He rolled around in the cornfield for a few minutes and, by the time he screamed himself hoarse, the other men were ready to tell Clint anything and everything he wanted to know.

"Mr. Timberman took them to the ranch."

"Why?"

"He wants them to sign over a quit claim deed."

Clint knew a little about the law. Not only would they have to sign a legal document, but it would have to be filed at the county court house before it was legal and binding. "First, where's the ranch, second, where's the county court house?"

The ranch was only about fifteen miles to the south and the county court house was in Bandolier. Clint and Richard had been there on several occasions. Clint looked around at the devastated cornfield and the cattle, which were already starting to wander back in hungry anticipation.

"Richard, see if you can get some of these men patched up enough to drive those cattle the hell out of this valley."

"You mean we just let them go?"

"Without guns, they pose no threat. Besides, I got a feeling they were just misled. Isn't that right, boys?"

The cowboys nodded their heads. "Just following orders is all."

"Next time, you better question your orders if you know what is smart," Clint said. "Richard, I'm heading for Timberman's ranch."

"I want to go, too!"

Clint was tempted but there were wounded men here who

needed bandaging. "You get the wagon and load up those that need a doctor. Drive into Bandolier and meet me there. That's where Timberman has to show up."

"He'll kill you both for sure," a cowboy said. "I just wish I could be there to see it happen."

"You might get your wish," Clint replied over his shoulder as he headed for his horse.

"Dammit, Clint!" Richard wailed. "I deserve to come along instead of playing nursemaid!"

"I know," Clint said as he bridled Duke. "But one or the other of us has to stay and make sure that things are done around here to protect whatever corn there is left standing. And since gunfighting is my business and yours is selling barbed wire, then the decision on who should go and who should stay seems pretty clean cut. I go. You stay."

Richard stomped on back to the wounded men. When Clint rode out, heading for Matt Timberman's ranch, the Midwesterner was ripping up shirts to make bandages. Richard Bates was very angry. But then, he knew that getting Priscilla and Margaret back was a job for the Gunsmith. And he also knew that he might still have a chance to be in on the showdown in Bandolier. All that was necessary was to hurry.

Chapter Twenty-One

Margaret was trying desperately hard not to swallow a gag that now silenced her completely. Without much strength remaining, she stubbornly worked at the knot that bound her wrist, despite the fact that she knew her struggles were hopeless. She had signed the quit claim deed just a short while ago when they threatened to kill her sister. Now, Margaret realized that Priscilla was still holding out and refusing to co-sign. This realization did not raise her spirits but, instead, had exactly the opposite effect. Priscilla had proven herself the stronger and the smarter. She had refused to believe Matt Timberman and his cruel men. Margaret felt crushed by shame and guilt. She felt like a betrayer as she listened to the conversation in the next room.

"Why can't you be reasonable and avoid any more pain?" Matt Timberman asked. "Your sister has already shown good sense by signing this document. Do the same."

Priscilla shook her head weakly. She had been punched, choked, pinched and mauled by Timberman's men for hours. It was dark, but she had no idea if it was before or after midnight. Priscilla only knew she could not hold out much longer. She felt as if she were about to lose contact with reality, and the room was starting to spin very slowly.

Timberman knelt before the chair she was tied to and grabbed her face. His thumb and forefinger bit into Priscilla's cheeks, but at least the pain stopped the room from spinning. "Just sign on the goddam line and we're finished. You and your sister will be free to leave."

Priscilla laughed, the sound of it chilling even to herself. "You'll kill us the moment I sign."

Matt Timberman was in his fifties, medium height and build with bushy black eyebrows and silver hair. He looked distinguished, but that was an illusion he took pains to create and maintain. In fact, he possessed all the refinements of a tom cat. He was vicious and greedy. He was also very intelligent and cunning.

"That's not true! And I've agreed to pay you well for that valley. Now, how would it look if you and your sister turned up dead or missing? Bad. Bad is how it would look. I can't afford that kind of thing. I want to be a state senator some day. No sir," Timberman said, "I want to pay you both a fair price for your homestead and see that you go back to wherever the hell it was that you came from."

Priscilla mumbled the words she had been repeating for hours. "I won't sign."

Timberman slapped her so hard she felt as if her neck broke. Priscilla lost consciousness for a moment and then a dipper of water was tossed in her face. She opened her eyes and saw that they were untying her from the chair. She decided that they had decided to kill her. Strangely, she was so tired and dispirited she almost did not care.

"We are going to take a nice long buggy ride into Bandolier. I'm going to the bank and I'll pay you in cash. You and your sister can leave Texas with more money than either of you would ever see on that homestead. You can go back home and be whatever you want to be. Two women alone do not belong on the Texas frontier."

Priscilla laughed harder.

The men in the room looked to their boss and their expressions showed worry. "Maybe she's going crazy," one said.

"She just needs a change of scenery," Timberman snapped. "Get the buggy hitched up."

"But you'll get there before dawn if you leave now."

Timberman did not like his orders to be questioned. "I'll have a woman alone in the buggy, won't I? If any of you men think I'm too old to appreciate that fact, you're making a big mistake. Besides, I want to be the first one in the door when the bank opens. I'll pay her and then we'll go over to the court house and make it all legal."

"You're wasting your time," Priscilla said through clenched teeth. "Nothing can make me sign."

"Is that right?" Timberman grinned. "I tell you what. If you don't sign, and if I have to come back here empty-handed despite all my trouble, I'll take your sister and use her until she's so ripe the dogs won't have her. How does that sound?"

Priscilla felt herself trembling. She was beaten and she knew it. "What guarantee do I have you'll keep your word?"

"Use your head!" Timberman snapped. "If you cooperate, I'll see you both to the stage with your money. You get to go home to Minnesota or wherever you come from, and I get your place and the water rights that go with it."

Priscilla nodded her head woodenly. "All right," she said, trying to believe that it was in Timberman's own best interests to honor his part of the bargain. After all, he did have political aspirations and she doubted that he would jeopardize them to save a few thousand dollars.

"Good," he said, his voice suddenly losing its hard edge. "I knew you were going to see things my way."

He turned. "Hitch that buggy up. Phil, you, Ed, Bob and Charley come along as outriders. There will be no trouble, but it pays to make sure."

The four men nodded. The one named Phil untied her wrists and when the blood flooded back into her hands and fingers, it felt as if liquid fire were pouring through her veins. Priscilla allowed herself to be supported by Timberman. He put one arm around her waist and the other slid up to cover her breasts. Priscilla was so weak and beaten she didn't even have the strength to push off his advances.

And as they half-carried, half-dragged her out to the waiting buggy, she wondered if Timberman would force himself on her. After all, what was to stop him? She was too weak to resist and he was apparently keeping poor little Margaret here at his ranch until she kept her part of the bargain.

Despite her resolve, Priscilla felt hot tears streak down her face. She had fought hard. When the men had come, she and Margaret had used their new-found skill with rifles to hold their attackers off for nearly an hour. They had prayed that Clint and Richard would come, but that had not happened.

Priscilla allowed herself to be lifted into the waiting buggy. The stars were shining in the heavens, but they were blurry because of her tears. She was sick to her stomach with dread about what the rest of this terrible night would bring.

Any way that she looked at things, she was going to lose.

Chapter Twenty-Two

Despite the fact that he was riding into danger, it felt good to be on a horse again. The night brought coolness, and the stars glittered with the sharp promise of danger. Clint wondered if this Matt Timberman fella had a bunch of professional gunnies on his payroll or just some rough cowboys to do his fighting. It made a big difference. Clint was not a man who liked killing and, in his experience, whenever most cowboys came up against a professional gunman, they quickly realized they were outmatched.

The Gunsmith touched his horse with spurs and the gelding responded eagerly. Mile after mile they traveled at a steady ground-devouring gallop. It was sometime near midnight when he saw the dark silhouette of the ranch house and the outbuildings. There were lights on in the house, and Clint knew that they would be waiting for him. He made a wide circle around the ranch and came in from the opposite direction. They might be expecting that, too, but it was worth a try.

Clint sat on his horse for several minutes as he carefully studied every detail of the Timberman ranch. There was enough moonlight to see the buildings outlined against the backdrop of the pale land. He studied the corrals, the barns, the workshops, and the bunkhouse. If he got into trouble, it was good to know where he was and where he needed to go. The ranch house was a single story affair with two wings separated by an open, canopied roof. The open part was referred to as a "dog trot" and it was the favored place during hot days and warm evenings.

Satisfied that he knew the most likely place that Priscilla and Margaret would be kept hostage, Clint dismounted and yanked his Winchester out of its scabbard. Chances were, if there was a gunfight, he would be relying on his six-gun, but if he were spotted before he could get in among them, he wanted a rifle's firepower. Clint tied Duke to a piece of brush and raced forward, keeping low to the ground and moving in a crooked line so that he would be a more difficult target. He headed for what appeared to be the blacksmith shop, and when he reached it, he flattened against its rough wall and caught his breath. He expected to hear the bark of a ranch dog, but there was none. That worried Clint. Most frontier ranches had four or five dogs hanging around; they served as guardians against surprise Indian attacks and had saved many a family or an outfit from total annihilation.

Clint wondered if they had penned the dogs up on purpose just to lure him into a trap. It was possible, but unlikely. Timberman would not have expected that Clint and Richard would be able to stand up against the men he had left at Priscilla's and Margaret's ranch. It would have been reasonable to expect that both of them were dead.

But the Gunsmith was a very suspicious man. He moved toward the ranch house with his rifle up and his eyes scanning every inch of the yard.

"Sic 'em!" a man yelled.

Clint glanced over his shoulder and saw two wolf-sized animals come racing from the bunkhouse. They were huge and when you saw dogs like that attacking without going through the nonsense of barking, you knew that they were killers.

Clint had no time to sneak up to a door and let himself in politely. He could hear the dogs panting and their footfalls sounded like running deer. He debated only about ten seconds as to whether or not he should turn and draw his Colt and try to kill both animals. But realizing that he would be a perfect target caught squarely in the middle of the yard, Clint decided his best course of action was escape. So he lowered his head and ran for his life, feeling the dogs closing rapidly in on him.

There was a window open, Clint could see the curtain waving outside. That was where he headed and, without even breaking stride, he dove through it with the two dogs right on his heels. All three of them crashed down on a soft bed and then the dogs were trying to tear at his legs. It was totally dark in the room and Clint knew that he was fighting for his life. He still had the Winchester in his fists and he reversed his grip on the weapon, grabbing it by the barrel. He swung blindly at the dogs and when he heard one yip and felt the stock of the rifle land solidly against the beast's skull, he took heart. Two or three more wild swings and then both animals were howling and leaping back out the window.

Clint leaned against a wall. His heart was thudding loudly in his chest and his breath was raging in and out of his lungs. That had been the worst so called "stealthy" approach on an enemy he had ever made in his life. The entire ranch knew he was among them, and they knew his exact position. There was no reason to play it cautious anymore. If the women were being held with guns at their heads, Clint knew that he stood damn little chance of saving them unless he attacked hard and fast.

Setting his rifle down, the Gunsmith drew his six-gun and groped his way to the door. He pushed it open and it was totally dark in the hallway. Something told him that he was walking into a crossfire if he stepped outside that door.

Clint hurried back to the window and climbed outside. He moved quickly toward the dog trot, and when he rounded a corner, he saw a man with a drawn gun peering down the darkened hallway Clint had almost entered.

"Looking for someone?" Clint asked softly.

The man started to swing his gun around, but Clint had already taken three steps and was bringing his pistol crashing down on the man's skull. The Gunsmith let the cowboy drop in the dirt before he removed the fellow's six-gun and stuffed it into his waistband. He studied the fallen gunman for a moment and happily concluded that he was not a professional.

Clint took the man's place and waited patiently. He knew where his enemies were and that was his single advantage over them. Five minutes passed, then ten minutes. Clint was in no hurry. He figured that there had to be at least four rooms facing the long hallway and, in one of them, he would find Margaret and Priscilla.

"Psssst! Ernie, where the hell is he?" a man whispered from the other end of the hallway.

Clint waited a moment but realized he had to say something.

"Dunno."

"Shit!" the man hissed. "He musta taken off after the dogs got to him."

"Musta," Clint muttered.

A block of light cut into the hallway as a door opened. The Gunsmith saw three men peer out of their rooms. He edged back from their sight and waited for them to come to him. And they would, sooner or later. In this kind of cat-and-mouse game, patience was almost always rewarded.

He heard the clump of boots on wooden floor and the door opened. There was enough moonlight to see silhouettes clearly, but not a man's features. "Ernie?"

"Yeah," Clint said, pulling his Stetson down tight.

"You didn't—"

Clint didn't know or care what the man's question would be. He used his pistol again to send another one of Timberman's cowboys crashing to the dirt. Then, he tugged his Stetson down close over his face and eased into the hallway. He moved down its length quickly and when he saw two men step into one of the rooms, he followed close on their heels.

In an instant, he saw Margaret and she was tied to a chair, a gag stuffed into her mouth. Their eyes met and it was a good thing that young woman was gagged, or she would have given her captors a sure warning. As it was, Margaret just made a sharp, gasping sound, sort of the way a chicken does when its neck is caught by a man's fist.

Clint's gun was out and he stepped back into the doorway. "I guess he didn't run away after all, friends. Now up with your hands and don't . . ."

A door slammed and Clint spun on his heel. He fired in a split second, and the man who had just entered the hallway crashed right back out the door. Clint knew the man was dead. He spun back around and with his gun leveled, he said, "Keep 'em up if you want to keep breathing."

There were four cowboys in the room and they all showed good sense.

"All right," Clint said, "with your off hands, reach across your bellies and unholster your six-guns, then move over to the wall and hope that I don't get an itchy trigger finger."

Clint waited until his orders were carried out before he went over to Margaret. He yanked the gag out of her pretty mouth. Before he could say anything, she blurted, "Thank God you've arrived! But they took Priscilla to Bandolier."

The Gunsmith was relieved. "That just means they need

her signature on the deed to your place. She'll be all right until then.''

''Where's Richard?'' she asked as he untied her, taking care that his gun never left the four cowboys.

"He's heading for Bandolier right now," Clint said. "I told him to lie low until we get there."

"But how did you know that Mr. Timberman would take her there?"

"Just a hunch," Clint admitted. "I knew that he'd have to show up at the county seat sooner or later. But the problem right now is what to do with these jaspers. I think maybe I ought to just shoot them and be done with the bother, don't you?"

As Clint said that, he had winked and Margaret understood.

"Might as well," she said with a shrug of her shoulders. "They sure aren't any friends of mine."

"Now wait a minute!" one of the cowboys said. "We did no harm to her! Ya can't just gun us all down in cold blood!"

"Sure I can," Clint said. "I done it lots of times. In case you haven't figured me out, I'm determined to help these women." He cocked back the hammer of his gun.

The cowboy and his partners went pale with unconcealed terror. "I swear we'll go away and never come back!" one cried. "There's no need to start pulling that trigger!"

Clint scowled. "I dunno," he said gruffly. "I guess if you boys was to grab your two friends I laid out cold in the dog trot, and if all six of you were to be off this ranch before sunrise, then I might let you live."

"It's the same as done," a cowboy said, not giving Clint a chance to think about it any further. "Let us past you and we're gone from here forever!"

"Then git!" Clint ordered. "You best run for it until you're out of sight of this ranch. I see any of you ever again, you're dead men, Is that understood!"

It was clear that it was perfectly understood.

Clint and Margaret followed the four outside and watched them heft the two pistol-whipped men onto their shoulders.

"No horses?" a cowboy asked, eyeing the dark vista of land that surrounded them like an ocean. "We could get out of your sight a whole lot faster."

"No horses," Clint said. "Just run for it!"

They broke and ran. It was almost comical how much effort they put into the flight. They were all wearing high-heeled cowboy boots and they wobbled. That, plus the fact that they were trying to carry two unconscious men sure did make it an amusing sight.

"How are we going to get my sister away from Mr. Timberman?" Margaret asked.

Clint shook his head. "That's the main question. How many men has he got with him?"

"Four."

"Professionals?"

"You mean, are they gunfighters?"

"That's exactly what I mean."

Margaret shook her head. "I can't be sure. But I don't think so. Maybe one or two of them are. How do you tell?"

"By their clothes. And the way they wear their guns at their sides. There are other ways, but you'd not have noticed."

Margaret was silent for a few minutes before she said, "Clint, how soon are we leaving for Bandolier?"

Clint watched the cowboys struggling into the deepening darkness. They'd have to come back to this ranch for horses. There was no hope for them in that vast country on foot without food or weapons. The question was, would they come to Bandolier or would they leave the county? Clint figured that he had scared them so badly they would keep riding.

At least, he sure hoped they did. They had not raped or beaten or even mistreated Margaret. If they had, Clint would not have been so lenient.

"Let's find you a horse and ride," he said when the cowboys struggled over a rise and disappeared. "Let's finish this up in Bandolier."

Chapter Twenty-Three

Bandolier was a bustling cattle town with more charm than most of its counterparts scattered along the western edge of the Texas frontier. It had been founded by A. E. Sedge, a hide trader who liked the setting so well he had built a small general store and saloon. During the first year of trading, Sedge had been forced to battle Comanche raiders at least six times, and somehow kept his scalp. He had finally made peace with them by agreeing to pay the Indians five good woolen blankets and a barrel of whiskey every month. It had been an equitable bargain on both sides. True, he had also had to pay the Kiowa an equal sum when they discovered his arrangement, but even doubling his monthly fee did not seriously cut into Sedge's profits.

Hides had soared in value and, within three years, Sedge employed no less than fifteen freighters to transport his smelly cargo to San Antonio. He had considered hiring buffalo hunters and skinners, but when a trio of hunters had threatened to slit his throat if he did that. Sedge had wisely changed his mind. He was no coward, but neither was he a fool. In fact, he was wise enough to realize that greed was often the cause of a man's downfall. Sedge was a simple man of simple tastes. He liked to spread the wealth around.

A. E. Sedge had died, poisoned by a whore who claimed

that Sedge had agreed to marry her until he had gone to St. Louis and brought back a "respectable" lady named Clara Bell as his bride. The whore had been convicted by an outraged jury then sentenced and promptly hanged from one of the many lovely cottonwood trees along Bandolier Creek. There were almost fifty people living in Bandolier then, and many of them wanted to change the name of their town to Sedge in honor of its founder. But wiser heads and opinions prevailed and the name of the town had remained unchanged. There was a plaque made and paid for by the town council. It had been nailed to the biggest tree in town, but someone had stolen it, and the town council had refused to buy a replacement.

The memory of A. E. Sedge and the millions of buffalo which had brought him into this country was quickly fading. Now, bold cattlemen and empire builders like Charles Goodnight, Oliver Loving, and Joseph McCoy were the new Texas legends. And if a poll of the citizens were taken, most of them would have figured that A. E. Sedge had really not done that much after all. He'd just been a wise businessman and left a rich widow and a whore to hang.

Clint had heard all this not-so-ancient background and history of Bandolier and had not bothered to mention to anyone that he had once saved Sedge's life. There had been a gunfighter named Baston who had decided to kill the old hide trader for his money. Clint had just happened to be in town and, being a lawman at the time, he had faced Baston and beaten the man to the draw. Sedge had paid Clint a hundred dollars and offered him the whore for a whole week for free. Clint, being a man who enjoyed both money and women, had accepted both offers and spent a wonderful seven days in the Bandolier Hotel. He remembered the whore as being surprisingly active in bed and prone to be possessive of a man's favors. If Sedge had asked him, Clint would have warned the man that the whore was certainly capable of committing an act of murder while seized with jealousy.

"What are you thinking?" Margaret asked as they rode toward Bandolier.

"About Sedge and his whore," Clint said.

Margaret frowned. "I don't know either of them and I don't think I want to know. But you ought to be thinking about Priscilla."

"Oh, I have been."

"I sure hope Richard has come."

"He will have."

"You aren't much of a talker, are you?"

"Only when I have something worth saying," Clint told the woman. "And right now, I'd just sort of enjoy some peace and quiet."

Margaret turned her face away from him, and they rode on in silence. Clint listened to the night sounds and smelled the oak and the dry grass. He was not sure what would happen in Bandolier. Things could always go wrong and when a man planned every little detail, then most always when it came to a gunfight, he would discover that nothing worked as it was supposed to.

"There it is," Margaret said in a rush of excitement. "I see the lights way off in the distance."

Clint judged the time to be around three in the morning. He was dog tired and knew that he needed at least a few hours' sleep to be quick and steady.

"Hey!" Margaret said when the Gunsmith reined in his horse and dismounted. "What are you doing?"

Clint loosened his cinch and then unsaddled and unbridled Duke. He did not bother to use hobbles because the black gelding was trained to stay close. "I'm going to get some shut-eye," he told the woman. "I suggest you do the same."

"With my sister in Timberman's hands! Are you crazy!

We can't stop out here on the range."

"We can and I have," Clint reminded the woman. "I suggest you dismount and try to sleep a few hours. Matt Timberman will be hiding someplace, and we'd never find your sister before morning."

"But what if he has . . ."

Clint knew why Margaret was so upset; she was afraid Timberman had raped her sister. Clint shared the same concern but did not want to show it.

"If he has, he would have done it by now anyway," Clint said. "There is nothing in the world we could do to help her tonight. The best thing I can do for your sister is be clear-eyed enough in the morning to handle trouble if it comes."

"How can you be so . . . so uncaring!" she cried. "You and Priscilla were . . . were sleeping together. I thought that you would marry my sister and live at our ranch."

"Uh-uh," Clint said, settling down for his sleep. "Your sister deserves a better farmer than I'd ever be."

"And a better man!"

"I sure wouldn't argue with you there either, Margaret. Now, could we sleep a while? It'll be daylight in only a few hours."

"I won't sleep," she said almost defiantly. "And I don't see how you can either!"

"It takes a cold heart," he said. "And a weak mind. Now, wake me when the sun rises about a foot off the ground. No need to do it any earlier than that."

She seemed speechless. Clint was glad. He just leaned his head and shoulders back against the wool underside of his saddle and closed his eyes. Within a minute, he was fast asleep.

Chapter Twenty-Four

Clint awoke with the sun in his eyes, and his first impulse was to roll over and go back to sleep. But the moment he closed his eyes again, he realized that something was wrong. Very wrong. It was far past the hour when he should have been riding into Bandolier.

"Margaret? Margaret!"

The woman was gone. Clint jumped to his feet and turned around in a complete circle. Duke was the only living thing he could see between him and Bandolier.

"Damn!" Clint cussed, grabbing his bridle and hurrying over to Duke, who had been grazing with contentment. "Dammit anyway! That fool woman went on into town without me!"

He slipped the bit between Duke's teeth quickly, then saddled him and, within minutes, was swinging onto the tall horse. This was not going to happen the way he'd expected!

Fifteen minutes later, Clint slowed his racing horse as he neared town. At the first hitch rail, he jumped out of the saddle and tied the gelding, then hurried toward Bandolier's only bank. He was halfway down the street when he heard an explosion of gunshots. Before he could even think about reacting, he saw Richard come backpedaling out of the bank with Margaret in tow. Margaret was screaming and the lead was flying.

171

Clint drew his gun. He raced forward just in time to see Richard and Margaret leap behind a water trough as bullets riddled it.

"Where's Priscilla?" he shouted.

Richard twisted around. His gun was empty, and he was ramming the spent cartridges out as fast as he could before reloading. When he saw the Gunsmith, he looked more than relieved. "She's inside with Timberman and his men."

"How many left standing?"

"Five."

"But that's how many there were to begin with!"

"I know," the Midwesterner yelled back. "They had Priscilla in front of them. I couldn't risk hitting her."

Clint moved into a good position and took cover. He was not exactly sure what the next move was going to be. Only that it would have to be Matt Timberman's.

Timberman was not a man of great patience. He pushed Priscilla before him and when she reached the door, he growled, "Tell those two to throw their guns down or I'll blow your brains all over the sidewalk."

Priscilla shook her head. "Shoot me! You will anyway."

Timberman grabbed her by the hair. "Tell them, I said!"

Everyone in Bandolier could hear Timberman's command. Clint swore silently and holstered his six-gun. He called over to Richard. "You stay behind cover. If they have us both, we're as good as dead."

"Let me go instead."

"I wish I could," the Gunsmith admitted. "But he wouldn't take you. Just stay put."

Clint stepped out into the street with his hands raised to shoulder level. "Timberman, let's make a deal."

"You don't have a damned thing I want!"

"Sure we do. We have twenty thousand dollars. We can make a swap."

Timberman rubbed his jaw. Maybe he realized that the entire town had heard his threat and that his political future was nonexistent. "Where's the money?"

"Hidden. But we can get it within an hour." It was a lie, but Clint knew that it was the only way to buy time for Priscilla.

"Get it! You've got just thirty minutes. In the meantime, I'm going to take this woman to the county courthouse and file a quit claim deed on her property. If you try to stop me—either of you—she dies. Is that clear?"

"Sure is," Clint said quietly. "Just relax and pretty soon you'll be twenty thousand dollars and a valley richer than you are right now. But if you kill her, you're the same as dead."

"You got twenty-nine minutes left," Timberman said. "Move!"

Clint turned and disappeared. He ran behind some buildings and then stopped to think. He knew that the county courthouse was at the east end of town. It was sort of off by itself and that was bad. If it were close in among other buildings, maybe he could have sneaked across rooftops or something and gotten very close. Close enough to have a chance at killing Timberman and his four gunmen.

Clint made a quick decision. He raced down an alley, and sprinting as hard as he could, he went flying into the county courthouse. Inside, there was just a single clerk. The man was about Clint's age, but that was all they had in common. He was thin, bespectacled and wearing an eyeshade. Incredibly, he had kept on working despite all the gunfire. When Clint crashed inside, the clerk looked up and said, "Can I help you?"

"Damn right you can! Give me that eyeshade and your jacket. Hurry up!"

"Who are you and what do—"

Clint bounded over to the man and ripped his eyeshade off. "Excuse my manners, but I haven't got time to answer your questions. And if I were you, I'd get out of here before the shooting starts."

The clerk took a long look into the Gunsmith's eyes. He nodded his head, shucked out of his jacket, and bolted for the rear door.

Clint shrugged into the jacket, which was at least three sizes too small. He yanked on the eyeshade and jumped into the clerk's desk chair, which, fortunately, faced the door leading to the street. He drew his gun and laid it down in his lap. He could see Timberman and his four men coming with Priscilla in front of them.

The Gunsmith felt his eyes sting with sweat. He mopped his brow with the sleeve of the clerk's jacket, and the motion tore out the right armpit. Clint did not even notice. This was going to be dicey as hell. Five men against one—no, make that three. Richard Bates was out there somewhere with a gun and so was Margaret. He'd taught them both to shoot quick and straight, especially Richard.

Clint hoped they would not fail him because in about three minutes, all hell was going to break loose in Bandolier.

Chapter Twenty-Five

Priscilla felt herself being shoved up the steps toward the county court house door as Matt Timberman said, "You had better act like you're signing over your claim because you want to, not because you have to. Understand me?"

Priscilla nodded. She had no choice. But no matter what happened to her, she knew that her sister and Clint were alive and would stay alive if she just followed orders and signed the quit claim deed without a fuss. Then, Clint would find the money, pay Timberman, and they would let her go. It wasn't good, but at least no one that she loved would die.

"I'll do whatever you say," she heard herself tell the man.

"Damn right you will." Timberman growled, as he shoved her up the steps.

The moment she entered the court house and saw the clerk, Priscilla knew it was the Gunsmith and that he had raced down here and somehow taken another man's place behind the desk. She stiffened, her plan of action suddenly no longer applicable to these new and explosive circumstances.

"Hey!" Timberman barked. "How about some service!" Gone was the façade of gentility he normally showed to the world.

Clint had a pencil in his left hand and was hunched over

an open ledger. He lifted his six-gun and eased it over the top of the desk so that the butt was resting on the spine of the ledger. And as Timberman's eyes grew round and large, the Gunsmith said, "You bet I'll give you service. Now raise your hands and—"

Timberman shoved Priscilla forward. Hard. She crossed the Gunsmith's line of fire and before he could squeeze off a shot, the cattleman and his four hardcases were jumping out of the doorway, scattering both to the left and to the right.

"Get down!" Clint yelled to the woman as bullets exploded through the front windows and set glass flying. The Gunsmith reached the door to see that Richard and Margaret had dropped two of Timberman's gunmen.

"Freeze!" Clint yelled, as he skidded to a halt in the street. "It's over."

But Matt Timberman felt otherwise. He had a gun in his fist and his eyes were wild with hatred. When he twisted and saw the man who had orchestrated his downfall, he screamed and fired.

Clint threw himself forward and when he hit the street, he rolled. Each full revolution he made counted for one shot that sent a bullet into Timberman's body. By the time Clint had stopped rolling, Timberman was folding at the knees and starting to crumple like a wet paper bag.

Clint swung his gun to bear on the last man, but the fellow threw his hands over his head and bellowed, "Don't shoot!"

The Gunsmith picked himself out of the dirt as Richard and Margaret disarmed the man and ordered him to lie facedown in the dirt. Then, Margaret and Priscilla were running to hug each other and cry with relief.

Clint yanked off his Stetson and used it to whack the dirt off his clothes.

"You're a mess," Richard said quietly. "If we're going

back to San Antonio, you're going to have to have a new set of clothes and a better hat. Wouldn't do to ride in looking like a range bum."

Clint grinned. "I guess you're probably right about that," he said. "But first, I need a drink, a bath, and a steak dinner."

Priscilla disengaged herself from her sister's arms. "And you need a good woman in your arms for one more night," she said, not ashamed of herself for those words. She knew that the Gunsmith was leaving, and she had accepted the fact. She hoped Margaret also understood that Richard Bates had to return to San Antonio.

"Yes," Clint said, "I sure do. Know of any 'good women' in Bandolier?"

She knew he was teasing her. "I might know of one."

Clint took her arm and headed for the nearest saloon. "You've probably never been inside the kind of place I'm taking you, and I don't expect you to ever visit one again. But I need a whiskey and they usually have a little sarsaparilla for boys and women."

Priscilla shook her head. She was still trembling. "I could use a real drink," she confessed.

"Hey!" Richard shouted. "What about him?"

Clint looked back at the man who had surrendered. "Ask him if he wants to share a drink with us and be friends," Clint said. "His boss is dead and this fight is over."

The man named Phil nodded his head vigorously. "Damn right I'll share a drink with you. And I'll do the buying!"

Clint hugged Priscilla. "See there, sometimes a little mercy pays extra dividends!"

Bathed, shaved, wined and dined, with a complete set of new clothes hanging off his bedpost, Clint felt like a lion as he slid between Priscilla's milky white thighs. He entered her with a powerful thrust of his hips.

She moaned softly, her fingernails making circles on his back as he began to move slowly around and around inside her. He pushed himself up on his elbows and looked down at her smiling face. "You'll find a husband as soon as you want to," he told her. "You're a hell of a desirable woman—in bed or out of bed."

Her fingers stopped moving, she stiffened a moment, then forced herself to relax. "I can't even think about another man right now."

"But you will, Priscilla. Both you and Margaret will."

Priscilla's eyes fluttered as her hips moved faster. She was already breathing hard. "I know this," she whispered, "I'll not settle for a man who uses me like a cow just for his own pleasure. I know how that feels. I want someone who can do what you do."

Clint chuckled. "Good luck."

Priscilla pulled his face down to her glistening breasts. She wanted him to suck on her nipples because that always sent her into ecstasy. Clint was more than happy to oblige. He took one, then the other into his mouth and enjoyed them as the woman began to thrash and moan. And when her legs flew up and she locked her heels behind the small of his back and began to buck like a filly, Clint knew she was coming.

"Hang on, honey," he warned, "because I'm going to send you flying higher than the moon."

Priscilla tried to speak, could not. Her eyes flew open wide, and she started to cry out, but Clint closed her mouth with his own. Then, he let her go crazy and just as she was stiffened and then went limp, he lost control and filled her.

San Antonio and revenge seemed trivial compared to what now lay quivering and panting under his hard body.

Chapter Twenty-Six

The day was warm and big thunderheads billowed up in the sky making the air sultry and humid. Flies buzzed and the brown Texas grass was shriveled dead. Before too many months, fall would color the trees, and there would be frost on the grass in the morning. Frost so thick that when you walked across the prairie, you'd hear your boots making crunching sounds with each footfall. But for now, the air was still, and Clint was perspiring heavily as he worked side by side with Richard.

"Are you sure you want to do it this way?" the Gunsmith asked, as he stared at the men and mules who plowed the field in preparation for planting corn. "Seems to me it would be a whole lot simpler just to ride into San Antonio and have the showdown. I like to get things like that over as soon as I can without taking foolish chances."

Richard Bates straightened from the work. "Not only will this serve as a warning to Duclaw and men like him that I intend to fence the West, but it will draw the opposition out to us. If there's to be a showdown, I want it to happen because they came to destroy my crop and the barbed wire fence we'll use to protect it."

"They'll come all right," Clint said as he helped Richard string the barbed wire. "Putting up this stuff just ten miles

179

north of San Antonio is like waving a red bandana in front of a Spanish fighting bull."

"Do you disapprove?"

Clint was wearing thick leather gloves but even with them, occasionally a barb would cut through to prick his flesh. "Not entirely," he said, studying the men with the plows as they marched back and forth. "This is good cattle country, and I suspect that, wire or not, it will always raise better beef than corn. But with cattle, you have a consolidation of power. A few get rich and stay rich. They become like feudal lords ruling tens of thousands of acres. But with farms, well, you have common men like myself raising families, building on their dreams. Going to church, raising barns, feeding chickens, and watching their kids grow tall and straight."

Richard laughed. "You're a farmer at heart! Don't try to deny it."

But Clint shook his head. "If I was a farmer, I'd have stayed with Priscilla. No, I'm ready enough to return to my gunsmithing shop and the easy life I led gambling and traveling around."

"It does sound good," Richard said. "But I think you'll be settling down before too many years. Maybe raise a few of those kids and chickens you speak so fondly about."

"If I'm lucky to survive the trouble that will be coming our way when they hear about this, you might be right," Clint said. "But let's get this fence up and we can speculate later."

Richard nodded and, while the Gunsmith strained to keep the wire taut, he pounded another staple into the post and fixed the wire tight. "This sure isn't my idea of fun," he said.

It wasn't Clint's, either. In fact, every time he thought about what they were doing and where they were doing it, he decided that he must have had sunstroke and lost his senses. Each day, cowboys trailing their herds would pass on by and some men, not recognizing the Gunsmith from a distance, would curse or jeer them.

Clint did not blame the angry cowboys. He was putting up barbed wire which would change their way of life. Alter it forever and probably diminish it greatly. But that was progress. Things were always changing. When one man profited, it was usually at the expense of another. Maybe with fences, a few cowboys would take up the plow, raise themselves families and find a better life. Cowboying was a very young man's game. Few could withstand the hard and dangerous work past age thirty. I wonder, Clint thought, where do all the cowboys go when their bones go brittle and their joints stiffen and pop?

It took them ten days to finish fencing the cornfield and then Richard announced that he had no intention of planting a crop—not ever. "It's just the principle of the thing," he explained. "It's just that I bought this quarter section of land which gives me the legal right to fence it if I want to. Besides, I have a feeling that, if I can keep the wire up, then others will feel they can do the same."

"The big cattlemen like Duclaw will understand that," Clint said. "And because they understand, they'll have to tear the fence down."

"I think they'll try to stampede it in the night," Richard said quietly. "I think that's what I'd do."

Clint did not understand. "If they couldn't do it in the plaza, then why should they think they can do it out here on the range?"

Richard smiled. "Think about it. At the plaza we had a hundred head of longhorns. And they scattered from the center so that there was no focus to their assault on the wire and posts. But with a thousand head of cattle all running in the same direction, they'll go through this fence like a bullet through butter."

"I see." Clint frowned. It made sense. He could remember how the fence posts had groaned and one of the wire strands had pulled loose. He realized that, until this moment, Richard's demonstration in San Antonio had made barbed wire seem almost invincible. And it wasn't.

"So now we oil our guns and wait," Clint said.

Richard nodded. "Yeah. We just sit and wait." He stared south toward San Antonio for a long moment then he added, "You know what?"

"What?"

"If I live through it, then I think I might go back and marry Margaret."

Clint was not surprised. Since leaving her, Richard had not quite been himself, though the Gunsmith figured some of his pensiveness and irritability was due to the fact that they were going to be attacked.

"Well?" Richard wanted a response. "What do you think of that?"

"Sounds like a smart thing to do," he said.

"Damn right it would be! But we'd not stay on the farm. We'd travel together. A man selling all the time is lonely. Besides, Margaret is a farmer's daughter. She could speak on how barbed wire saved her cornfield."

"Sounds like you've put a lot of thought to it," Clint observed.

"I have. It's my observation that the wives of farmers have considerable say in things. Sometimes, they even make the decisions."

"Amazin'," Clint said drily, for he had made a similar deduction years ago, only it applied to the whole female species.

Chapter Twenty-Seven

Richard had been correct about how the attack would come. It came at sundown with the rolling drum of thousands of hooves.

"Here they come," Clint said, moving purposefully toward his black gelding. With almost a sense of relief that the waiting was over, he quickly saddled and bridled the horse but did not mount.

Richard took another full minute. He drew his rifle and expelled a deep breath when he saw the huge herd of cattle being driven toward his fenced field. "I feel sorry for the leaders of that herd, Clint. When they hit the wire, it will tear their legs out from under them. They'll be trampled to death or end up crippled and having to be destroyed."

"Let's just hope we're around to put them out of their misery," the Gunsmith said tightly. Clint also drew his own rifle, knowing that he would need it for less than ten seconds before he switched over to his handgun. They had jointly decided to lay their rifles across their saddles and fire from cover until the cattle hit the fence. After the pileup, they would mount and ride into the dust and confusion and take their chances. "Get ready to fire."

Clint laid his cheek down against the stock of his rifle and took aim on a man riding point. He squeezed off a shot and saw the rider take the impact of his bullet in the shoulder.

The man lost a stirrup and fell, but he was far enough out to the side of the stampede so that he wasn't trampled to death. Others were less fortunate. Clint and Richard laid down a withering fire as the cattle crashed into the barbed wire fence. For a terrible moment, the wire held, then the posts broke and cracked like dry twigs. Wire screeched like a fighting eagle as it was torn from its staples and then disappeared under the stampede. But even though down, the wire exacted its toll on the longhorns. Clint saw a full line of the leaders crash to the earth, flip head over heels to vanish under the onrushing herd.

"Here they come for us!" Richard shouted.

Clint shot two men who charged forward, and Richard emptied another saddle. It was good shooting. Clint slammed his Winchester into his saddle boot and vaulted onto his horse. "Let's finish this off!"

He and Richard spurred their horses forward as riders emerged from the dusty confusion, the flying cattle, and the thundering hoofbeats. Clint and Richard met them bullet for bullet. Quite often they missed, for the light was failing, and it required a little luck as well as skill to hit anything from the back of a racing horse.

But as they sliced into the rear of the herd, shooting until their guns were empty and then grabbing spares from their waistbands, they suddenly felt rather than saw the opposition break. One minute there were riders coming at them with guns blazing, the next minute the riders were turning their racing mounts away and vanishing in the swirling dust and confusion.

They broke through and the herd swept past them. It churned through the soft, plowed fields and then galloped mindlessly into the falling darkness.

Richard and the Gunsmith pulled their horses to a

standstill. Both animals were badly winded, and Richard's mount had taken a nasty gash from a horn to its flanks.

"Is it over?" Richard shouted.

Clint dismounted. "Almost," he said, walking his horse back toward the fence, stopping at the body of each fallen rider and making sure that there were no survivors needing medical attention.

He came to Duclaw's body. The cattleman was lying face-down in the dirt and when Clint pulled him over, his expression was one of shock and surprise. A rifle bullet had gone right through his chest.

When Clint came to where the barbed wire fence had been, he again withdrew his rifle and, together with Richard, they shot the crippled longhorns. At least, Clint thought, there were no good cowponies on the ground.

Richard had become very quiet. And when the first evening star appeared, he said in a shaky voice, "I don't think I realized how many men were going to die to protect my rights. We killed seven, Clint."

"I know." Clint reached inside his saddlebags and produced a bottle of whiskey. "Change always comes hard in the West, Richard. Hard, and generally with men and animals getting hurt or dying. But they were grown men, and they came to run us out, trample, or shoot us, whichever was easiest. We can hold our heads up when we ride back into San Antonio for the undertaker."

Richard Bates nodded. He squared his shoulders and reached for the whiskey Clint offered. "I know," he whispered, "but I sure can't wait to see Margaret again."

The Gunsmith understood. He had been in this kind of situation before and it never got easy. But a man stood for what he believed in and he fought the best he could when others gave him no choice. Some of Duclaw's riders had given him a choice when they'd turned their mounts during the charge and fled; those that had not were now dead.

Richard choked on the whiskey. Clint climbed into his saddle. "Come on," he said wearily, "let's ride for town. In a few days, you'll be going to see Margaret and maybe . . . maybe I'll tag along for a while."

Richard forced a smile. "I'd like that," he said fervently, "I'd like that one whole hell of a lot."